1 897709 21

ABLE SEACAT SIMON

Simon is discovered in the Hong Kong docks in 1948 and smuggled on board the HMS *Amethyst* by a British sailor who takes pity on the malnourished kitten. The young cat quickly establishes himself as the chief rat-catcher in residence, while also winning the hearts of the entire crew. Then the *Amethyst* is ordered to sail up the Yangtse, and tragedy strikes as it comes under fire from communist guns. Many of the crew are killed, and Simon is among those who are seriously wounded. With the help of the ship's doctor, the brave cat makes a full recovery and is soon spending time with the injured men in the sick bay, purring and keeping their spirits up. Soon, news of Simon's heroism spreads worldwide — but it is still a long journey back to England . . .

ABLE SEACAT SIMON

LYNNE BARRETT-LEE

ISIS
LARGE
PRINT

First published in Great Britain 2016
by
Simon & Schuster UK Ltd.
A CBS Company

First Isis Edition
published 2016
by arrangement with
Simon & Schuster UK Ltd.

ISBN 978–1–78541–256–1 (hb)
ISBN 978–1–78541–262–2 (pb)

Published by
F. A. Thorpe (Publishing)
Anstey, Leicestershire

Set by Words & Graphics Ltd.
Anstey, Leicestershire
Printed and bound in Great Britain by
T. J. International Ltd., Padstow, Cornwall

This book is printed on acid-free paper

In memory of all who served aboard
HMS *Amethyst*

And our own little Alfie
RIP

Author's Note

From the moment I was asked if I'd like to tell Simon's story, two things became immediately clear. First, that I would say yes, without a moment's consideration, and second, that it would be a labour of love.

After all, how could it not be? I love cats. I love writing. I especially love writing while in the company of my cats. So, to write *as* a cat? What could be nicer?

And what a joy it has turned out to be. But, unlike most of the novels I have written in the past, it also involved an element of responsibility. For all that this is fiction — a re-imagining of a famous naval incident — it was vital that I remain true to history. Not so much the small, day-to-day things, because that would be impossible, but to the memories of both my doughty four-legged protagonist, and to those of the men with whom he served.

It goes without saying that I have done much research. I've read books and testimonials, pored over maps, charts and photographs, tried to familiarise myself with "jackspeak" and naval lore and ship parts, and welcomed the word "corticene" into my life. It's obviously my hope that the book wears this lightly — with enough verisimilitude to capture the moment but sufficient innocence that a small, skinny, black and white kitten feels very much the narrator of the story.

However, what I've mostly been is humbled. Like

Simon, an innocent in matters military and nautical, the more I immersed myself in the horror of the Yangtse Incident, the more awed I became. It's already well-documented that the *Amethyst*'s young crew returned as heroes, and that many were duly decorated, and rightly so.

But, as is often noted when it comes to momentous events, in order to fully appreciate how it *felt* you probably had to be there. And though I lay no claim to that — I was only there vicariously — my need to "be" there, in the sense of getting to better know these brave seamen, has helped me understand what they went through on a much more personal level.

I hope I've done them justice (and that they'll forgive me putting words in their mouths) because I could not respect or admire them more.

PART ONE

PART ONE

CHAPTER
ONE

Stonecutters Island, Hong Kong, May 1948

I'd finally found a good route across the island. I used the same one every day now, and could have walked it in my sleep. Past the tamarinds, down the passage past the big house and the small house, across the road, mindful of traffic (which could strike you down and kill you), along the side of the big sheds where men clanged and banged a lot, then down past the cranes onto the docks.

The rain will come, kitten. That's what my mother had always told me. *It will come in spring, and it will teem, and it will fill the air and drench us. It will drip from your whiskers, and it will plop from your eyelashes, and it will get in your ears, you wait and see. It will come down so hard that it will dance before your eyes, kitten, and you'll be wet through. And, trust me, you won't like it one bit!*

I had never seen rain then, not a single glistening drop of it. Only the dew that collected and sometimes fell in streams from the banyans, and the sea, which lapped gently on all sides of where we lived. So while I did trust my mother, and believed everything she told me, I couldn't quite imagine what rain would feel like. As with so many things I'd experienced since I'd lost her, I was to discover there were still a lot of everyday things I didn't know; not just the mysteries that lay beyond the harbour.

Today, though, I didn't need to imagine. I was wet. I might even, I supposed, be wet through. I was heavy with wet; "wet" clearly being a thing to be concerned about, just like strangers and traffic and snakes. A thing that streamed from my eyes, made my paws slip and slither, made my underbelly cold and damp and dirty. I could see it dancing in front of me, just as she had promised — kicking up from the lakes it had made of all the alleyways, jumping up and down on all the wall tops and roofs.

It was raining, so it must by now be spring. The time when my mother said the world would start changing. The time of warmth and something wonderful called "plenty". Which was good, because there hadn't been much plenty since I'd lost her. So far, I had only been able to catch just one or two mice. And that was then. Before hunger. Before spring. Before rain. And, weak from the pain that gnawed and clutched at my stomach, I didn't know if I'd ever catch anything again.

I slipped through the spaces between two sets of fences, wondering when life might get better. If I didn't manage to catch anything, then what would become of me? Which was why (I kept telling myself this, over and over) I'd had no choice but to go down to the docks and scavenge for scraps, despite all that my mother had told me — repeatedly — about how dangerous it was to be around humans.

The quayside was an assault on all my senses, as always. The big ships with funnels, the smaller ships with sails, the swarms of running people, the shouting and whistling, the sudden metallic shrieks and clangs, the gouts of steam and smoke, the cargo crates and nets swinging high above the ground. I felt my mother's presence keenly as I approached my special spot: the place where she'd explained the rudiments of hunting and where I, always distracted by the wonders all around me, took too little notice of the skills she'd tried to impart.

My ears pricked and I tipped my nose a fraction higher, sniffing. Could I trust this one smell among the many, many odours? I slunk down into the space between my usual barrels with great care, and rounded the corner to where food sacks were often piled up — there to be loaded, my mother had said, onto the ships bound for the sea.

And then I stopped, transfixed. Because perhaps today was going to be a better day. For a few yards in front of me was a shrew. I knew it was a shrew from the shape of its snout. *Look first*, Mum would say to me. *Don't just leap in haste. Look.* So I lowered myself down, not even caring about the wet now, just the tiniest fraction of the tip of my tail twitching, because that, my mum had told me, was what a tail was meant to do.

The shrew had so far been lucky. Something bigger — a rat or a fox or a cockatoo, even — had nibbled its

5

way into the corner of a sack of grain. It was the bottom-most sack of a pile among many piles; piles that reached way higher than I was. The shrew was feeding, preoccupied, rooting around with its back to me, and, as far as I could tell, had no ready means of escape. The first surge of strength I'd felt since the rain had come coursed through me. I'd have that shrew, I just *knew* it, for my dinner.

Everything went wrong in an instant. So wrong that something else my mother had told me popped into my head. Was this going to be a day for misadventure? Her words came back to me, as they always did when things became scary: *remember,* she'd say, *every day holds the capacity for adventure, kitten, but never forget that it holds the capacity for misadventure too.*

And it looked like misadventure might have found me. I'd been settling into position, just a moment from pouncing, when a sound and a strong smell hit my ears and nose together, and a voice — a deep human voice — broke the spell.

"Well, well, well, well!" it said. "What do we have here, then?"

The still-lucky shrew streaked away out of sight, but I realised I had no such possibility. Not without turning round, and I knew I mustn't do that. So, instead, I arched my back, and I hissed.

The human — a man — opened his mouth again and laughed at me. "Hey, little feller, don't be scared. I won't hurt you."

I hissed again, drawing my lips back, partly in rage, partly in terror, all the while trying to work out my own best means of escape. Should I make a leap for the nearest barrel? Scale the sacks just ahead of me? Try to squeeze myself through the tiny space by the wall, as the shrew had? It was clear from the way the man was still looking down at me that he wasn't going to leave me alone yet.

"Hey, kitty, kitty," he said, looming even closer, squatting down on his haunches and extending his arm.

I knew about this. Sometimes humans liked to offer things to you and then, when you plucked up the courage to inch closer, would grab you and take you away and put you in a cage. My terror intensified as soon as that thought popped into my head, because I knew all about cats being put in cages. It was probably only because I was still a kitten that I hadn't yet been in one — because putting kittens in cages was considered bad luck.

But perhaps the human in front of me didn't know about bad luck, so I shrank further back against the wall and hissed at him a third time.

Again he laughed. "Don't be scared, little feller. Don't be frightened." And then he reached all the way to me and just as I tensed, stricken, he smoothed his huge human hand all the way down my back, like the kind lady in the big house used to do.

"There," he said. "My, you're just skin and bone, aren't you, Blackie? Shall I see if I can find you something to eat?"

Eat. He meant food. And I was starving, so I wavered. But most humans weren't like the lady in the big house. I knew that too. I saw my chance. Spied the sack. Made a leap and scrabbled up it. Then ran away just as fast as my legs could carry me.

CHAPTER
TWO

I never knew what happened to the brothers and sisters who'd been born along with me. My mother never said, and I was too scared to ask, for fear of hearing something that would frighten me. Cats were supposed to have nine lives — it was one of the first things I ever remember her telling me — but even so, one by one, all of them had disappeared. "Such a shame," the lady in the big house used to say, shaking her head as she stroked the tips of my mother's ears.

And now they had gone too, both the kind lady and my mother. I couldn't help wonder why I'd worried so much about hearing about my brothers and sisters, because now that I was completely alone in the world I'd have liked to know what had become of them. And, besides, being afraid of almost everything now felt normal.

Fear travelled with me everywhere because there was so much to be frightened of. It had almost become something of a friend. It accompanied me on all my hunting forays, curled up with me wherever I hid myself away to sleep, whispered in my ears as I prowled around the island, trying to keep to the secret places and shadows.

I knew fear was a good thing, that it would help keep me out of danger, but it was beginning to be such a constant and insistent companion that there hardly seemed room for anything else. But I was a kitten, soon to be a cat, and there was something else still burning bright in me — the curiosity that I'd been born with. And that night, as on most nights, as I padded along the jetty, it was still up to the stars that I looked, rather than down to the planks beneath my paws.

It was midnight. And, bar the gentle slip and slosh of the waves, silent. The noise of the harbour always lessened as the moon rose, almost as if it had been instructed to do so. Just now, the huge orb was low-lying and lemony, but I knew it would soon rise up to take its place among the stars, becoming smaller and brighter and whiter.

Bathed in its glow, the city of Hong Kong was transformed. By day full of the sights, sounds and scents of human industry, by night, from my vantage point at the far end of the jetty, it seemed a less scary, more pretty place altogether. One strung with distant lights, where diamonds danced on the water.

This is our time, my mother had often explained to me, as we'd sit and gaze out over the inky expanse together. *The time when the humans are all going to sleep. The time when the moon is our friend.*

I had liked the moon then. I liked it even more now. Moonlight always seemed to me the friendliest light of all — particularly now that she had left me. The starlight, too, from stars that every living thing had originally come from. Stars to which the soul of every cat always returned.

I took up my usual position and curled my tail around my paws, feeling the breeze tickle my whiskers and the salt prick my nose as I watched the water lapping lazily at the jetty's wooden pillars. Then I gazed up, imagining my mother up there somewhere, looking down at me. Remembering how, a while before she'd been run down and taken from me, she'd told me that she would always be there, watching over me, whatever happened.

I'll be enjoying my ninth life, she'd told me, which had initially confused me. So she'd explained that cats were lucky. Perhaps the luckiest of all the creatures. Because our nine lives meant more than perhaps I'd imagined; the eight on earth, which was why cats could afford be so curious and courageous, and then the ninth, up in the stars for all eternity.

I gazed at the moon, wishing eternity didn't feel quite so far away, then padded back towards the beach, in search of prey.

Prey was always on my mind but, as hard as I tried, prey kept managing to elude me. By the time the dawn broke on another day I was so weak with fatigue and hunger that the dock, with its slim promise of scraps to pick over, seemed once again the only place left to go. At the very least, I knew I could find a sheltered spot in which to rest before trying again.

So I returned, trying to pad my way lightly along the soggy paths and alleyways, always on the lookout and alert to new scents but, bar a brown snake that reared up and hissed at me threateningly, still failing to find anything to pounce on. But it wasn't just my empty stomach that was drawing me back. Despite my knowing what my mother had said about how dangerous it was to show myself, the memory of the kind man I'd met the day before had stayed with me. And as I slipped once again through the holes in the fences, I kept going back to what he'd said. Did he really mean me no harm? Could I trust him? Might he feed me? Despite the danger, I wanted to find out.

When my mum had still been with me, I'd been curious about everything. So much so that there had been many times when *she'd* been the fearful one. When my curiosity might well have got me into trouble, had she not been there to remind me of all the hazards in the world. I was curious again now.

And the more I thought about the man's kindness, the more I wondered. Had I been right to run away from him after all?

Yes, of course you were right to run away, I could hear my mother's voice telling me. *Who knows what might have happened to you? Humans are dangerous.*

But a part of me — a guilty part, even as it was a defiant part — kept thinking *no.* Because it seemed to me that not *all* humans were dangerous. Snakes were dangerous. Rats were dangerous. (My mother had had a scar on her nose to prove it.) Cars and trucks were extremely dangerous, as was everything else that travelled so fast and so threateningly along the big road. I knew I wouldn't forget about that, ever.

12

The old woman in the big house hadn't been dangerous at all, though. Yes, she'd been human, but she'd given us food and been kind to us; those were two of my earliest memories. Milk on a patterned saucer. Little morsels of meat. She'd also been the last human to stroke me. To bend right down to stroke me and say, "Look at you, with those little white socks on your feet! Now, don't you be going getting them dirty!"

I threaded my way along the quay in the hope that, in this at least, my mother was wrong. And as I walked, I wondered how life might have been if the old lady hadn't vanished from our lives the way she had. If the man with the dog — our most mortal enemy — hadn't moved in there instead. If we'd not had to run away from him quite so fast.

"Well now, you're back again, are you?" The voice was loud and close and clear. But not such a fright now, because today I had expected it.

The quayside was once again bustling and noisy, gangplanks slung down from ships like so many giant tree creepers, disgorging sailors and fishermen, deck hands and mess boys; and stern men in hats, who dodged different men in different hats, cursing and chattering, weaved their heavily laden wooden carts in and around and between.

From my vantage point, hidden in the gap between two oil drums, I had curled up and watched him for a bit. He'd come, I realised, from one of the tallest ships currently docked there, and was today, like the rest of the men that teemed around it, dressed differently from previously, in polished shoes and crisp navy kit. Their white hulk of a ship, which had been tied up for some days now, had a tall mast, and two pairs of guns that pointed forward, which I knew were used for something called war.

The man stood in the ship's shadow and considered me. He then looked around, and strode off, his shoes clicking rhythmically, and, before I had even stretched my paws out and yawned, had returned, holding something in his hand.

He squatted down on his haunches again and held it out to me. "Sardine," he said. "Well, a piece of one, anyway. Freshly caught this morning."

I drank in the aroma that began to engulf me. I could almost taste it. "Go on, little feller," he urged again. "Help yourself."

I wanted to. Badly. The smell was almost hypnotic. But I hadn't been so frightened since the last time I'd been chased — by the dog at the big house, who'd nearly caught me. And curiosity was one thing from a safe spot between two sturdy oil drums, quite another when you were standing out in the open, close to a human, and your heart was pounding almost out of your chest.

I lifted a paw. Took a step. Cautiously sniffed at what he was holding out to me. But my instincts were too powerful. His movement towards me was only very slight, but still enough to have me skittering anxiously away.

"Here, then," he said, laying the piece of fish on the ground in front of me. "Only grab it quick or the gulls will have it before you can say knife."

14

So I grabbed it between my teeth and bit down on it ravenously, all the while backing away towards the space between the oil drums. It would be terrible if a gull *did* steal it, because I'd never tasted anything quite so delicious in all my life — or so gloriously without fur or feet or whiskers! I was so engrossed then (almost in heaven; so much fish at one sitting!) that when he reached out to stroke me this time, I didn't flinch.

Though *he* did. "Gawd, kitty, there really *is* nothing of you," he said. "Is there? Poor little mite. Where's your mum, eh? You a stray? All on your lonesome? You poor little blighter. Look at you shaking! Shhh, now. Don't be scared. I won't hurt you, I promise. You know what? I've got one just like you back in Blighty. Well, like you, but there's a good deal more of 'im than you, for certain."

"Hickinbottom!" Another voice rang out, and this one did scare me — not least because, at the sound of it, the man whipped his hand away, snapped back to his feet and spun around.

"Aye aye, sir!" he called back, stiffening. "Over here, sir! Just coming!"

"Good. Because there's two dozen potato sacks here that won't shift themselves, Hickinbottom!"

"I'd better go," he whispered. "You enjoy your breakfast, little Blackie."

And with that he was hurrying back across towards his ship.

CHAPTER
THREE

"So there's dry stores, and wet stores — and those big sacks over there, Blackie? They're all the veg that'll be going in the vegetable bins down below. Then there's the tins. Loads of them to load. Corned beef and kippers. Chopped ham. Potted chicken. Feed the brute! That's what they say. You enjoying that?"

It was the following morning, early, and it had dawned dry and warm. And I'd greeted the sun with a full belly. I had caught a mouse in the small hours, and my joy knew no bounds. Neither did the gratitude I now felt towards my new friend, the sailor who'd given me the fish that had given me the energy — not to mention the confidence — to make my first kill in days.

And now *another* sardine. This time a whole one, which he'd already told me he'd "half-inched", whatever that meant, from the stack of crates near a fishing junk further down the quay.

"Polish it off quick," he'd said, and I was obliging him by doing precisely that while he puffed on a cigarette and lifted his face to the sun, apparently as pleased to see it smiling down on us as I was.

I should have known that there was going to be something different about today. I was a kitten, after all, so I was supposed to be good at sensing things. But I didn't. Perhaps because of the fish, which took up all my attention, or perhaps just because I was so happy about my earlier catch. Either way, I wasn't prepared for what happened next.

I was cleaning my whiskers, looking around for a puddle of water I could perhaps lap from when the cigarette end was flicked away and the sailor's hand reached down to stroke me. Or so I thought. Instead, his hand wrapped right around me and the next thing I knew was that I was being borne aloft — up, up, up, up! — and was held there, high in the air above his head.

Terrified, I pinged my claws out. Then I mewled at him and furiously scrabbled my back legs against the inside of his wrist. He just laughed, pushed his cap back, and lowered me down a little, now holding me, legs dangling, closer to his grinning face.

"Steady on, Blackie," he said. "You already *know* I'm not going to hurt you." Then he brought up his other hand and cupped it around my head, flattening my ears. "Shhh," he soothed, "shhh," even though I wasn't making any noise now. Not so much as a hiss. I didn't dare to. "No need to panic, is there?" he reassured me. "No need at all. Look, you even like it," he said, rubbing the fur under my chin.

"Look, you're purring. See? I'm not so bad, am I?"

I didn't know about that. How on earth could I? This was a *human* who was holding me, and that should never, *ever* happen. Not even the lady in the big house had picked me up, *ever*. She wouldn't have dared to.

My mother would have gone for her. But he had just picked me up and held me like I wouldn't mind at all.

And that was the funniest thing. Despite my mother's lessons clanging loudly in my ears — *Never trust. Never touch. Never let a human lure or grab you* — I found I actually didn't mind him holding me. Which was no sort of thing for a kitten to be thinking. Not a kitten who valued all nine of his lives. It was at exactly that point, just as I was enjoying being cuddled, that I realised I might have made a terrible mistake.

No, not "might", I decided, as his grip on me tightened further. *Had* just made a terrible, possibly fatal, mistake.

"You know what, Blackie?" he said, lowering his voice a little, and confirming my worst fears. "I reckon you'd fare a *lot* better coming with me than staying here." And with that, I was suddenly gripped even tighter, and plunged into the fusty darkness inside his shirt.

If I'd been frightened before, I was petrified now. The assault on my nose was the first thing — it was shocking. I'd never felt such an intense, frightening animal smell before. If that wasn't enough to make me wriggle and squeal in terror, the lack of air, the furious rub of my whiskers against what felt like his skin — and *other* whiskers, the total blackness, the huff and puff and thump of his own breathing . . . it was all I could do to not succumb to the powerful instinct to claw and scrape and bite my way free.

18

Yet some other instinct stopped me. It was inexplicable, but it prevailed. I don't know if it was the constant firm but gentle pressure of his hand against my flank — now back outside the fabric that contained me — or just the voice in my head that had brought me back to him at the docks. Either way, it reassured me that he *wouldn't* hurt me. And as we hurried (for we were definitely hurrying) to wherever it was that he was taking me, the scared part became, if not exactly less scared, more pragmatic. I'd made a choice. I'd been curious. And if my curiosity killed me? Well, then, so be it. After all, why had cats been gifted all those lives if not to use them?

"Here we are!" the man called Hickinbottom whispered, just as I was bracing myself for whatever was going to happen to me. "Be it ever so humble, there's no place like 'ome!"

Then he chuckled, causing the whiskers on his chest to jiggle against me and gusts of that strange human odour to prickle in my nose. I was glad to be fished out from under his clothing and plonked down in front of him, not least because there was a great deal more air for me to breathe. Though I was now so stunned that it didn't even occur to me to run away. He rubbed my chin again, with a little finger, looking pleased with himself. "Welcome to the *Amethyst*, little feller," he said, pushing his cap back from his forehead. "And my humble abode. It might not look much, but you're honoured, you know. These here are *very* superior accommodations for an ordinary seaman, I can tell you. On account of me being Captain of the Fo'c'sle, you see. I get all this to myself —" he waved an arm around the tiny space he'd brought me into — "because it's my job to make sure everything's shipshape and in good order. Which is why I get berthed up here —" he jabbed a thumb behind him — "right up front, next to the captain's cabin. And you, me little feller, get first-class accommodations as well. Well, at least for the moment," he added. "I dare say you won't want to stay cooped up with me for long; be all over the place like a rash before we know it."

Having no idea what sort of "accommodations" might be classed as inferior, I looked around me to get a sense of where I was. On a ship, in the harbour — that much I'd already worked out, and everything I could see around me definitely bore that out. White. Everything white. Just like the ship was on the outside. Everything straight lines, hard angles, sharp edges. Cold to touch, most likely, both to the nose and to the paw. And a faint metallic tang in the uncannily still air.

But where he'd placed me felt particularly, well, peculiar. I took a tentative step, and was immediately frozen in fear again; for the grey ground beneath me, which seemed to be made of some kind of matted hair, felt almost alive under my paws. I tried to get my balance, which was no easy feat. And just as I'd done so, the man called Hickinbottom slung his cap down beside me, sending tremors once again beneath me. And I wondered, pulling a memory from somewhere in my brain, if we were already rolling on high, stormy seas, of the kind Mum used to tell me stories about. I pinged my claws out and hung on for dear life.

"You daft 'a'p'orth!" Hickinbottom said, placing the flat of his hand beside me, then pressing it into the softness a couple of times and watching me wobble once again. "This here's me hammock," he explained. "Me bed. It's where I sleep. And, if you behave yourself, little Blackie, you'll be sleeping here too. Though right now I need to stow it, quick smart," he said, scooping me up and plopping me down on the floor, "or the old man up there will have my guts for garters."

To my quiet satisfaction (because cats were supposed never to be wrong about anything) the floor I'd been put down on fulfilled all expectations, being slippery, unyielding and cold. Still, now I was here and fairly certain the man called Hickinbottom meant no harm to me, any lingering anxieties about what might become of me — I had, I supposed, been officially kitnapped — were buried beneath what I could only describe as a feeling of happy recklessness and glorious potential; I was on a ship, bound for the ocean and certain adventure. To a life beyond the island I had only ever dreamed about. Despite having so many reasons to be terrified, I couldn't help but feel my spirits soar.

Well, to a degree. If I thought too long, it was also very easy to remember that I was a very small, not-quite-yet-fully-grown animal, that I was alone with a human in a very confined space, and that I seemed to have no visible means of escape. I couldn't help but wonder how such little birds and animals as the ones I *had* successfully stalked must have felt when I had had them gripped between my teeth or claws.

So I did the sensible thing, and tried not to think too much about that, and to instead remind myself of all the good things that might come of this, and the kindnesses the man called Hickinbottom had already shown me — to try to focus on the excitement I couldn't help feel about everything being so different and new.

"Come on, move yer harris, Blackie," he said, interrupting my philosophising. He appeared to be engaged in some unfathomable and complex manoeuvre, requiring a number of very strange contortions. It was hard to be sure, but he seemed to be trying to turn the thing he called his bed into what looked like something else altogether, though whether he was achieving it was anyone's guess.

So, to be obliging, and because I definitely didn't want to be stepped on, I quickly scuttled out of harm's way, squeezing myself into the space between two strange metal objects that protruded from the wall, from where I could both keep an eye on his progress and take a proper look at the place I would also call home till such time as he decided it would be safe for me to venture out again. Though how long that would be, I had no idea.

"Right, that's me done," he said, finally, tugging at his tunic. "They'll be weighing anchor soon so I'd best be skedaddling. I'll be back in a bit, with some food."

Then he was gone. He was gone for some time, as well; time that I spent making circuits of the strange, tiny space, investigating every last inch of it. That done, I spent an even longer time washing my fur, and then monitoring the progress of a tiny, flitty fly, which, evidently much too high up to be concerned about my presence, went quietly about its business; something that seemed to involve bobbing back and forth just below the ceiling, and often knocking into it, for whatever reason flies did such kinds of things.

And it was fine. It was pleasant having no pressing need to go anywhere (though, as for needing to "go", I had to be judicious about that, opting, after some indecision, for a clean, obvious corner). I was happy enough, because I had grown used to enjoying my own company. Even before my mother died, I'd already known that I would have to leave her eventually, because the life of a cat was generally a solitary one, out of both nature and necessity. Cats — or so she'd told me — needed something called territory. Because cats didn't really like sharing.

I didn't know about that because it was a concept I'd yet to experience. It did make me think of the home I'd now left, though, and to wonder if I'd ever likely see it again.

But not for too long. Within moments, I was asleep.

Since it felt like particularly bad manners to keep my new friend awake half the night while I explored, I spent my first night as a seafaring cat doing what my mum had always told me was the answer to many a feline problem: I curled up at the end of the thing

George slept in and was soon far away inside my head again, chasing moths.

It had been a day of rest but, for all that, some exciting discoveries too. I discovered that sardines could come in tins — little metal containers, opened by little metal keys — and that they tasted even more sardine-y than normal sardines did, which was quite a revelation. And also good, because it seemed that sardines were another thing of which there were apparently "plenty".

I also discovered a thin white liquid, which George told me was called milk. He'd brought some with the sardines, and the taste of it took me straight back to a memory I'd almost forgotten. Of my early kittenhood, and of being so close to my mother that remembering the feeling now was almost painful. And via the milk, I also found out that George was called George, because the feeding of me seemed to invoke a memory for him too. Of the cat back at home, which he'd mentioned at the quayside.

"George! Is that cat up in bed with you again, you rascal!" That's what his mother would often say to him when he was younger and would sneak the cat — who was called Sooty, and who he told me he missed very much — into bed to keep his toes warm in the winter.

Knowing that made me sleep all the better in this strange new metal world, because it was so nice to know I was already being appreciated. But George's ship seemed to pay scant regard to the dreams we were both enjoying, because we were suddenly jolted wide awake in the darkness by a din so close and deafening that for some seconds I wondered if I was trapped in an oil drum that was being beaten with a stick.

Though, happily, I was soon reassured. I knew these strange whistling noises, I realised. I'd heard them often down in the harbour, back when I would spend the later reaches of many a night hoping the dark and quiet would lead to an abundance of prey.

It rarely did, as I still had so much to learn about stalking, but the moonlit routines had become familiar. The night insects gathering in the pools of brightness around the floodlights, the bats that would wheel and swoop and try to pick them off — not to mention make me wish that I, too, could fly. The sooty smell of the charcoal from the night watchman's brazier and then, often, when the bigger ships were moored, the meandering humans, who would sway and bump into each other and shout as they made their way back to the quay, and to their beds. "Don't fall in the drink!" they'd cry, "I'll bloody swing for her, so I will!", "Hey, just you mind your ruddy language!", and other incomprehensible babble, which would now perhaps start to make sense to me.

And then the pre-dawn cacophony, also human in origin, that started up long before the birds. A din that would begin even before the sun peeked over the horizon, with the clanking of bells and the squealing of pipes and the great wall of sound that was unlike any other; that of humans, many humans, being roused from their slumbers, and not liking it one little bit.

All this happened now; all of it simultaneously and all of it deafening (the ship's bell, I would learn, being particularly close). The combined clamour caused George, previously inert, to jerk and judder, and caused me, curled up tight in the warm space between his ankles, to shoot my claws out and cling on to the shifting grey mass beneath me, for fear of being launched into space.

"Yeeooow!" he yelled. "Streuth, Blackie! Jesus and Mary! Come 'ere. Gi's me legs back, for Gawd's sake, you tinker!" Then he plucked me from the covers, with scant regard for my still being attached to them, and nuzzled my cheek into the hot skin of his face.

"Aww, little feller," he said, his breath gusting warm and close, causing me to mewl at him. "This is nice, ain't it? Almost feels like I'm back at home. Don't be scared." (Which I wasn't, just somewhat stunned, which felt reasonable under the circumstances.) "You'll have to get used to this kind of racket, matey." He popped me onto his lap and ran his hands down my flanks, and as I luxuriated in the simple, rhythmic pleasure of being stroked by him, it hit me that perhaps I'd discovered something good. Something my poor mother might never have found.

That perhaps a cat's life didn't need to be solitary after all.

CHAPTER
FOUR

I learned so much in that first couple of days. I learned that it wasn't terribly nice to be in a confined space with one's toilet, and that the long hours between George coming back to check on me and feed me could grow almost intolerable to the nose.

I learned that the sea was an even more shifting mass than George's hammock; that sitting on the hard, polished floor of his tiny quarters was no protection from the feeling that if you stood up, your legs wouldn't quite behave in the way that your brain had been expecting them to.

I learned that the resultant queasiness (which had taken me completely by surprise, given how much the sea had always seemed a soothing, lapping presence) was one that was decidedly unpleasant, and that the only escape from it was sleep.

So I did a lot of sleeping, which must have been good for me, because I'd never felt so strong and rested, and with the anxieties of how I'd fill my belly removed at a stroke, it was the kind of sleep that came very easily.

Though I did feel scared at times. I couldn't help it. When you've lived with constant fear, as I had since my mother had been taken from me, you couldn't easily stop being fearful. And I knew I was right to be fearful about what lay beyond the fo'c'sle. Because, despite my instinct — that George was kind, that to be here with him was a good thing — I couldn't help think about my mother's many warnings about the lives cats like us should probably try to live. On that she had been clear, and with what had always seemed good reason: that, apart from the old lady, (who, even so, we should only approach with caution) we should keep away from, and be always wary of, humans. I couldn't help wondering every time I found myself itching to explore further, did my mum die because she was too curious a cat?

On the surface of things, no — she died because of the man who moved into the big house, and his dog. Because she was chased away from the one place where we felt no harm would come to us; because she ran, petrified, unseeing, out into the road. But her words dogged me, even so. I must keep my wits about me. Gentle George was one thing, the enormity of this huge metal vessel — and all the humans contained in it — quite another. I'd be a foolish kitten indeed *not* to be scared.

Even so, the itch to roam soon took precedence over the fear, not least because it seemed George was keen for me to explore, too. Since that first morning when we'd sailed, he had not locked me in, and it occurred to me that as he'd told me what a fine ship's cat I'd make I should better acquaint myself with the ship. So on the third day, George having been "mustered" "on-deck" (which I had by now worked out always involved him "skedaddling" away at high speed) I decided it was time to venture out.

The *Amethyst* was a place like no other I had ever encountered. Admittedly, in my short life, I had not encountered much, but here was somewhere — and something — that was completely unlike anywhere I'd ever been. Though its exterior held no surprises — I'd watched so many ships coming and going that the sight of a ship was very familiar — the inside of my new home was a mystery.

Like so many human structures, the ship was a box, but unlike the cavernous warehouses into which I'd sometimes sneak in search of sleeping lizards, it was divided into lots of smaller boxes. The junction between each box was also very clear. Where I was used to squeezing myself into slim gaps *between* things, here it was all about ups and downs. To get from one space to another, as I found out almost immediately, it was necessary to first leap over a small metal wall. It was complicated to understand, being so full of things that made no sense to me; within each new place that my tentative travels took me I saw the same lacework of piping over all the walls and ceilings, the same inexplicable lumps of wood and metal, all rising up from the same, highly polished red floor. It couldn't have been more different from the green softness I was used to seeing, or even the giant scale of all the human-made structures of the docks. It was so much to take in, in such a small, confusing space. I could only trust that I would begin to make sense of it eventually, and in the meantime not get hopelessly lost.

I saw no one. It was true that I hadn't travelled far yet, but this surprised me almost as much as it relieved me. Then I realised that the humans here must *all* have been "mustered" — the whole lot of them; a thing I would doubtless also learn about in due course. For now I was content just to explore my immediate surroundings, and to try to make sense of my strange new abode. Though finding my way outside, back to where I would be able to see the sea again, took some time and some doing, and some retracing of my steps, because there seemed little logic in the way the ship was laid out.

Back on the island, with its many meandering pathways and alleyways, it was simply a case of following my nose and eyes, and padding along, taking heed of the information from my whiskers. Up a slope, down a hill, through a space between railings; there wasn't much in the way of obstacles that could effectively bar my way. In this strange place, however, quite apart from the multitude of strange little barriers I must hop over, there were also step-ladders everywhere, which looked fine to scale, but far less appealing to descend. It was clear that, though to look at they were quite different, these had all the same qualities as trees.

Trees, as any cat would tell you, were never to be trusted. Trees were bewitching, confounding and ultimately deceptive, as I'd found out as a kitten of maybe not quite five months, when in bold pursuit of a large gecko. So easy to climb (a determined kitten could shimmy up one in no time) but, once there, it was almost impossible to get down. And my mother — this being a while before everything went wrong for us — seemed to find my plight very funny.

There is a reason you'll never see a cat up a tree, kitten, she'd observed, as I'd trembled and mewled and miaowed high above her. *It's because every cat recalls the day they did just as you have. Now, don't panic. Be brave. Trust you'll land the right way up. Land hard, yes, but the right way. You'll see. Come on, try it.*

She'd been right. It had taken half a morning, but she'd been right about both things. That I would land the right way up — even if only after a terrifying, uncontrollable, claw-shredding downward scramble. And that I wouldn't forget it. I vowed I would never scale a tree trunk again.

I elected to avoid the ladders too, at least till I'd worked out how I might negotiate them. So it was via a rather circuitous route that I finally found the outside, and when I stepped out there at last, treading lightly and cautiously, I realised I must have arrived at what George called "on-deck". Though there was no sign of anyone — which "on-deck" had he been mustered to? — I knew because for the first time in many, many hours now, I could smell salt and feel a familiar breeze caress my fur.

Being apparently alone — the shiny ground stretched into the far distance in both directions — I drank it all in, noticing how much the air differed from that in George's space in the fo'c'sle, which was air like no air

I'd experienced before, being so thick with dense, alien, often startling odours.

It was also fully light — a glorious morning, in fact — and I felt in no rush to explore further yet. It was enough just to look around me, take it in, letting my nose and whiskers reassure me, then cast my gaze upwards towards a sky so bright and butterfly-blue that I had to narrow my eyes in order to properly see it.

But it seemed I wasn't the only one "on-deck" after all. "What the very *devil* do we have here?" boomed a voice from behind me. "A cat? How's a ruddy cat found his way aboard my ship?"

Every cat's life is precious, so instinct prevailed. I dug my claws in — though into nothing, so that wasn't much use to me — and made myself as big and threatening as I could. Which I fully realised wasn't very big, much less very threatening, but I was too frightened to think rationally.

Except perhaps the dark part of my brain *was* being perfectly rational, because the other option, of running away, felt foolish in the extreme. Where exactly would I hope to run *to*? For what struck me most forcibly as I trembled beneath the human — tail fluffed, back a half-moon, teeth bared, teetering on tippytoes — was the sight, in the gaps between the deck edge and rail, of sea, and more sea, and not a great deal else *but* sea. The time for escape was clearly long gone.

And, just as George had, this human — this huge, thunder-voiced male human — seemed to find my predicament very funny. He also wasted no time in reaching down and scooping me up, though he grabbed me not by my belly, but by the scruff of my neck, just as my mother used to do. He brought me close to his face then and dangled me in front of it, breathing his man-scent (another assault on my nostrils as well as my dignity) and eyeing me just as I might have done a shrew.

For a moment, it was all I could do not to panic. One thing cats don't do for pleasure is swim, particularly in waves bigger than they are. Given the way he'd just spoken, overboard was where I must surely be headed. I'd have wriggled, even knowing the futility of it, but the scruff of a neck is a singular location — by some clever trickery, which I'd thought was known only to mother cats, I was entirely unable to move.

"Hmm," said the captain. (I knew he must be the captain, because only the captain would call it "my ship".) "A stowaway, eh? Or did someone smuggle you on board, eh?" He studied me intently for a number of seconds, as if seriously expecting me to answer.

I sniffed him. He smelled markedly different from George, which seemed appropriate, because George, I now knew, was still only a man-boy. I knew because of his "bum-fluff", as he called it, and his sharp observation that we were both of us teenage "waifs and strays", give or take, causing me to wonder if we weren't both in the same situation — both without our mothers, and neither of us feeling quite ready.

This captain was clearly no man-boy. He was a man and I could smell it, in the same way as I was always alert to the scent of the big cats on Stonecutters Island, in whose territories I never dared tread. His scent was earthy, and salty, and strong in my nostrils, though also strangely reminiscent of the shady spaces on the island where the jacarandas dripped their purple petals. "Well," he said, "since you are here, you may as well come meet my number one." Upon which, I was relocated to the crook of his other hand, and carried up and down the step-ladders I'd slunk beneath before, my heart beating out a tattoo against his palm.

"Weston!" he boomed (as I would soon learn was the way of things with captains). "Look what I've found promenading down the foredeck, bold as you please!"

He put me down on what seemed to be a sort of ledge, and, just as had been the case down on the deck, I took the view that to make a bid for escape would probably be pointless. Besides, I had not yet been thrown into the sea, so I suspected (at least, I hoped) that I might not. Though I could certainly see the endless glassy expanse of it, having now found myself in the place that must be from where the captain ran the ship.

Every cat likes a high place (as long as it's not a high place in a tree, of course) and this was a very fine high place indeed. It was right at the front of the ship, with a kind of windscreen to protect me from the stiff ocean breeze. In time I would realise that dozing behind it on a sunny day was a particular pleasure, but right now I was more excited by the awe-inspiring view; from up here, you could see right to the distant horizon; a place my mother always told me was special indeed, because that was where the earth met the stars.

Reassured now (the captain would surely have launched me overboard by now if he'd wanted to) I began to wash my nose and whiskers, both because they'd taken something of a battering on the scent front and because I was keen to make the best impression I could.

"Well, isn't that the darndest?" the man called Weston said, lowering a pair of what I would learn were called binoculars from his face, and shaking his head. "I saw this little feller on the quay the other day, and I was only saying to Frank that we should get ourselves a ship's cat. Well, I say cat. This one's only a kitten — not even a year old, I reckon."

My ears twitched hopefully. George had said exactly the same thing! The captain nodded. "Perhaps less. But he's a handsome little fellow, isn't he? Plucky, too. A bit small and scrawny, but if he's a stray, which I suspect he must be, that's only to be expected. And you know what they say about the strays round these parts, don't you? He'll probably make an excellent ratter."

I stopped cleaning my whiskers so the captain could stroke me, pushing my face tentatively up into his palm. It was a curious thing, this stroking humans seemed to like to do. Curious and nice, and I could feel myself purring. I'd hardly purred since my mother had died; it was like a muscle I had no use for. Yet here I was, astonished to find myself purring all the time, even when I hadn't exactly meant to.

I wasn't sure what a "ratter" was, but I had a hunch what it *might* be. This was confirmed when he explained that it was a very important post, for which he suspected a cat like me would be particularly well qualified, dispatching the vermin that were what he called one of the "most damnable evils of life in His Majesty's Navy", as they pilfered from the stores and munched their way through anything that took their fancy. "Or, rather, *did*," he corrected. "Perhaps no more, eh? Not when they get wind of this little chap in their midst!"

I decided I liked the captain very much, and would endeavour to do my very best for him.

"He'll need some meat on his bones then, sir," observed the third man, who had a face full of creases and very blue eyes. "Shall I call down and have one of the mess boys bring him up something from the stores, sir? Some herrings, perhaps. I imagine he'd be very keen on herrings."

"Absolutely," said the captain, plucking me up again for another inspection. "He'll certainly need feeding up a bit, if he's to be given a commission. And you'll need a name, I suppose, little chap," he added, to me. "An official ship's cat needs to have a suitable name."

"Socks?" suggested Weston. "Or Felix, perhaps? Tiddles?"

The captain rolled his eyes. "*Tiddles?* You hear that, Frank? Really? He'd really have me striding about the place, yelling 'Tiddles!'? I'd never live it down!"

"Alright, Korky, then," Weston suggested. "As in Korky the Cat. Now that would be apt, given the markings on him, wouldn't it?"

But the captain, though looking straight at me, seemed to be looking somewhere else, too. Somewhere

I had a hunch might be a good bit further away. "Simon," he said eventually. "I think we'll call you Simon."

"*Simon?*" Weston and the other man said simultaneously. "Why on earth Simon?"

"Very long story," replied the captain, very shortly. "And once you're fed, perhaps you can accompany me on my rounds, eh, little Simon? Weston, did that maintenance detail make a start on the boilers yet?"

Weston nodded.

"Excellent," said the captain. "So once you're fed, we'll start in the engine room, then, shall we, Simon?"

"Though you'd better take care not to let Peggy see him on your way down, sir," the man called Frank said.

"There's a point," said Weston. "He's right, sir. Better not. You know, I'm not sure if she's so much as even *seen* a cat before. I suspect she probably hasn't, don't you?" He, too, came across and stroked me. "Hmm," he said. "And I wonder what *you'll* do . . ."

"What they'll *do*," the captain corrected, "is to learn to rub along together as best they can. Just as we all do, eh?"

He put me down again and, having nowhere else in particular I'd rather be, I stayed where I was, wondering what sort of foodstuff a herring might be. And, more pressingly, wondering who or what Peggy was. They called her "she", so perhaps she was a lady, like in the big house. I hoped so.

More intriguingly, it seemed I was going to be called Simon now, as well as Blackie. And I thought I could probably live with that. I was learning lots about humans, and the curious words they used for things. And given it could have been "Tiddles", which, for some reason, had a bit of an unsavoury tang to it, I thought I'd probably got off quite lightly.

CHAPTER
FIVE

I soon forgot all about Peggy. And with hindsight that was probably understandable. There was so much for me to see and do — much of it in the dark hours of the night time — and the *Amethyst* was a very big place.

We'd been at sea a few days, and while the view of the horizon was largely unchanging, every day (and night) was still full of wonder because there was just such a lot to try to understand. The ship's routines, for starters, which I was beginning to get quite a feel for. And quickly, too, because, though I still spent plenty of time napping in gentle George's hammock, now the captain had discovered me I had become something of a novelty; so much so that on that very day he assembled the crew on the quarterdeck, and made my position on his ship official.

George had told me I'd be made welcome, and I was. He'd told me sailors had always had a friendship with cats, because cats kept sailors safe, having miraculous powers that could protect them from dangerous weather. He also let me know that sailors generally were a very superstitious bunch, and that if I walked up to one of them, they'd feel lucky. Of course, the flip side of this was that if I walked *away* from them, they'd be *unlucky*, so I might want to think before deciding to do that. He also told me (though while assuring me he didn't believe such nonsense) that back in the "olden days", whatever they were, some sailors also believed cats had storm-repelling magic in their tails.

Best of all, however, was the news that if anyone considered throwing me overboard they would think twice, because throwing a cat overboard would cause a great storm to sink the ship and kill everyone and should any lucky ones survive they would have nine years of further bad luck to look forward to.

In any event, it was all rather good news, I decided, as was the captain's announcement that he was giving me a "roving commission" as an ordinary seacat, with my number-one duty — as well as the bringing of luck and magic — being to take control of all the vermin.

Quite apart from all that, the captain seemed to have taken a shine to me personally. He would tour the decks, whistling, and it soon became obvious that sometimes he was whistling specifically for *me*, as I'd often hear him calling out his name for me as well. This put me in mind of the old lady in the big house on Stonecutters Island, and the way she'd often whistle to call my mother. It also reminded me of the affection she'd always shown us, and how my mother had once told me it was a cat's way to reciprocate, and to return such a compliment wherever possible. (Even if I knew full well that, in her book, such feline displays of affection definitely didn't include allowing yourself to be picked up and hugged, much less slung over a naval captain's shoulder.)

I would therefore always hurry to wherever he was and show myself, and he would express such delight at my having come "at his command" that I made it my business to hurry to him any time I heard him calling "Simonnnn!", or whistling for me to come to him. And it wasn't just because of the ease with which he could find me sardines, either. I was equally delighted to have made a new human friend. I thought perhaps my mother would have been, too.

Making friends very soon became the order of the day because it seemed everyone on the *Amethyst* wanted to say hello to me. Wherever I went I was greeted with the same affection George had shown me back on Stonecutters Island, and I quickly got used to being picked up and cuddled.

It was a very different life from the one I'd been living in Hong Kong. But I was still my mother's kitten and, for the most part, her words of advice still made sense to me. I would do as she'd always advised when it came to relations with other creatures; return the friendship my new human friends were extending to me by becoming the best ratter in the Navy. And so what that I lacked experience? I would make up for that easily — with enthusiasm, dedication and courage.

It felt good to have an ambition. To be given a role in life. To strive for something more fulfilling than just survival. And I couldn't wait to get underway. There was just the one detail that was holding me up. In order to kill the ship's vermin, first I had to track them down. And in this I still felt woefully lacking in skills or experience, bar half-remembered snatches of half-remembered information from my mother — that fresh rat's urine was so revolting that it made your whiskers shiver, and that they scuttled around the most at dawn and dusk.

So it was that on the fourth or fifth night after getting my orders I was still prowling optimistically below the waterline at dawn, having had what was shaping up to be a very productive night — my first true lead in what had become a rather lengthy campaign.

Ever since I'd joined the crew, I'd been trying to work out where I might find the promised enclave of marauding rodents, but up to now I hadn't had a great deal of success. I could often smell them (fusty and musty, like mice, only more so) but that had been as far as I'd got. Which didn't surprise me. If they were one of the evils — indeed, the very curse — of His Majesty's Navy, it seemed sensible to assume they were as crafty as any rodent, and knew their way around a ship a lot better than I did.

I also wondered if they'd got wind of my own presence. I'd only encountered rats very fleetingly, as one of the rules my mother had been at pains to have me heed was that I was forbidden from having anything to do with them. She had been clear in the utmost on how much danger a rat posed to a kitten; I was too small still, too weak, too inexperienced and too curious, and she assured me that when the day came when she deemed me no longer all those things, she would be the first to tell me.

Not that I'd even fully understood what she'd meant. That last bit, for instance. *Shouldn't* cats be curious? Wasn't that what cats were supposed to be? As a kitten, it had all been such a puzzle to me. In what way could being too curious about something as lowly as a rat pose a danger to a rat-hunting kitten? What could a rat — just a big mouse, really — actually *do* to me? They were grain-nibblers. Scurriers. Made for footling, not fighting. Whereas I had the tools for an altogether different kind of life. Speed and stealth. Grace and agility. A predator's teeth and claws.

And then I'd met one for myself, back on the island, and though I was only little then, I was *still* not convinced. Because my memory was not so much of a terrifying adversary, as of being a bold, courageous kitten, cruelly thwarted. That what I'd spotted had been a rat had been without question. Fat, dung-coloured rump. Scaly tail, like an earthworm. Unquestionably a rat — just like a mouse, only bigger — and I couldn't have been more excited. And having spied it scuttling away (another thing rats are good at), I simply did what a kitten is naturally compelled to do. I sank down almost to my belly, took aim, rehearsed my pounce in my head and then —

"*KITTEN, STOP!*" My mother's hiss pierced the air with such force that the entire rat, already aquiver, completely left the ground. And once back in touch with it, streaked away as if propelled by a hurricane, to go on and live — and to steal — another day. And I'd been cross — just as any thwarted kitten had a right to be, in my book. Humphing and harrumphing and generally mewling my displeasure at what she'd done. Oh, how I sulked! Till I was finally chastened by my mother — by her explaining at great length that a rat was, in reality, *not at all* like a mouse. That the fat-bottomed rodent I had set my sights on killing could just as easily turn around and kill *me*.

I trusted my mother, so was still slightly nervous as I padded along the passageways in the bowels of the *Amethyst*, nose up, whiskers twitching, reading the air. For all that the captain had assured me that I'd make a very fine ratter (though how could he *know* that?), my mother's stern warnings couldn't help but nag at me and neither could the memory of that scar on her nose. So the business of whether I was yet big enough, strong enough, experienced enough to deal with one — all of those were the questions I had yet to resolve. Without her to tell me — because she'd died before that day she'd mentioned happened — I would just have to judge for myself.

I was in no doubt about one thing — that I *must* be curious. I knew I'd be ratting no rats otherwise. Without curiosity, I would fail to even *find* one. The *Amethyst* was a place of secrets, a place of nooks, crannies and corners. Many of them places, presumably, where my human friends couldn't go — which was why rats, evil scavengers and skulkers in shadows, could set up home there and take things that weren't theirs. And as the captain's ratter — which responsibility I took extremely seriously — it was down to me to seek and find them, to get into all those places and (with luck as well as courage, both of which I knew I would need a lot of) take control, thin their numbers, make kills.

It was with that very much in mind that I stalked my first ship's rodent, which I came upon, finally, in the space between the flour sacks and pipes, at the very back of the dark, silent stores. It was its route I noticed first. I knew all about routes. This route was a rat run if ever I saw one. And though I could hear my mother tutting as I thought it, I thought it anyway; that it was *exactly* like a mouse run only bigger.

The evidence was clear. The husks of grains, the crumbs of bread and swede and carrot. The foul-smelling pellets that rats, being entirely without hygiene, drop thoughtlessly, randomly, disgustingly, in their wake. Then that odour — that once smelled was never forgotten odour — which was now making such an assault on my nostrils that it was almost like a magnet, reeling me in . . .

And then the prize, as I slipped round the edge of a metal bin. The rat itself, with its back to me, front paws up to whiskers; those whiskers twitching in a way that a cat's whiskers *never* would, rhythmically, quiverishly, furiously — marking the movement of jaws that were munching on food it had no business munching, that it had absolutely no right to steal. The captain had been right, I decided, as I watched it — it was the very curse of His Majesty's Navy.

I sank down slowly, feeling my belly fur almost melt into the floor beneath me, adjusted my position, and counted out heartbeats in my head. There was time, there was space, there was no way of escape for it. Two more heartbeats. Luck and courage.

I pounced.

The rat spun around, a blur of pale pink, black eyes and frantic whiskers, the spoils forgotten as it tried to scrabble claws at my face. But it was too shocked to do any more than slightly unbalance me, which — being a cat and *not* a rat — I quickly corrected, making firm, decisive contact with the side of its neck till its thrashing began to ebb and finally ended.

I waited, crouched and motionless, a full half-minute more till my heart slowed, my fur settled and the moment seemed right finally to relax my jaws and drop my prey between my paws. And it was only then that I began to appreciate just how heavy it had been. How one fat-bottomed rat had so much more bulk about it than a vole or a mouse or a shrew. How my mother had had a point when she'd cautioned against kittens taking them on. But I'd done it. I couldn't believe it, yet I'd really done it. I'd killed it. I'd dispatched it for my captain and could not have felt more proud. I'd become big enough and strong enough and would soon be experienced enough. I couldn't wait to take it to his cabin.

And I would have done so, except that fate intervened, and it seemed that someone else was destined to see it first. It was while I was on my way up top, moments later, that I bumped into him.

I was hurrying, keen that I should present it to the captain warm, and (I don't doubt, since I was feeling particularly full of myself) trotting along with something of a swagger. It was perhaps that which caused the sailor (who appeared round a corner out of nowhere, a massive man-shaped silhouette) to place his hands on his hips and make such a noise about it.

"Well, looky here!" he boomed, his voice echoing off the walls and the ceiling (I mentally corrected myself; the bulkhead and the overhead, of course). "Look. At. *You!*" he went on, seeming almost as proud of my kill as I was. "What's that you've got there, Blackie? Is it what I think it is?"

He stepped nimbly over the small metal wall beneath the door between us, moving into the pool of what little light was left burning at that time of day. He had a piece of paper in his hand and a pencil behind his ear. The light gleamed on his teeth as he grinned down at me.

He squatted in front of me to make a closer inspection. "Good Lord, it *is*!" he exclaimed. "What a clever little Blackie. Earning your keep already, I see!" Before I could take any action to evade it, I was then "treated" to a scratch of the space between my ears, which, with some effort, I just about tolerated.

It wasn't that I had anything against him — as with everyone I'd so far befriended on the *Amethyst*, he looked nothing but overjoyed to have had the chance to meet and stroke me. But it's no treat for a cat bearing prey to be touched. (Not even, might I add, by their mother.) It's quite the opposite. And try as I might to believe that he didn't mean to take the rat from me, certain feline instincts are way stronger than logic. Though I managed not to growl at him. Just.

But he seemed to understand anyway, because he stepped aside and made a dramatic sweeping motion with his arm. "On your way, sailor," he said. "Don't let me hold you up. And if it's the boss you're after, you'll find him on the bridge if you hurry. Blow me," he finished, now scratching his own head, using the pencil. "And you such a titch, and all, Blackie! Fancy!" Then he laughed. "Peggy'll be looking to her laurels!"

Even then, I didn't pay it a great deal of attention — either to the business of who Peggy was, or what "her laurels" might be. I was much too focused on the business in hand. Well, more accurately, the business at that moment in *mouth* — a dead weight between my jaws that was getting heavier by the moment, and that I had still to present to the captain.

As it was, I failed to find him, because he wasn't on the bridge and, fearing the man up there — Lieutenant Berger, who was apparently not a "cat fan" — I slipped away again, carefully, holding my head up as I went, so the rat's scaly tail didn't drag on the floor.

To the captain's cabin, then, I decided, but he wasn't there either, and it occurred to me that he might by now be back out on deck, doing the dawn "mustering" that seemed to bring him such joy. Since it seemed a bit presumptuous to waltz up with it while he was busy giving orders, I decided that the cabin was the best place for my trophy. I sprang up to his bunk and left the body where I knew he'd appreciate it — on the pillow.

It was only when I jumped down and headed back to the rat runs that it occurred to me. I still had no answer to my question. Who or what *was* this Peggy, anyway?

CHAPTER
SIX

When you live on board a ship, as I very quickly came to understand once I'd joined the *Amethyst*, life is all about order and routine. This obviously holds true for every drama a ship might encounter, but it's equally important on those days when there *is* none; those long days of ploughing steadily through the water, the sky above, the ocean below, the view calm and unchanging. That's where routine apparently makes for "good order", which was something the captain seemed to mention a lot, along with "shipshape", which seemed relevant, even if not entirely obvious, and "Bristol fashion", which meant not a jot to me.

But whatever the reason Mr Bristol had decreed it, his way of fashioning things created routine and structure, which made it quite unlike any day in my previous life. Back then, every dawn could bring entirely new challenges, many of them challenges I felt ill-equipped to face. Here, every new day was a copy of the one that came before it, and also a blueprint for the one coming after — each one so like the other that they soon began to blur; it would be only the ship's log that would enable any distinction to be made, and some specific memory be pinned to it.

With one exception. The day I met Peggy.

News of my first kill seemed to blow through the *Amethyst* like a hurricane, and I made even more friends as a result. It seemed the captain hadn't been joking when he'd told me what a scourge the ship's rats were, because the first thing he did was congratulate me fulsomely. "Well, thanks VERY much for my gift!" he said, chuckling as he did so. "What a TREAT it was to find it just before I had my breakfast! Absolutely DELIGHTFUL," and lots of other jolly things like that.

Everywhere I went, I was treated like a hero; applauded, roundly cheered, and given all sorts of food treats. In fact, the only dampening detail in the joy of my new status was that now I'd done it once I must of course do it all again.

And again. And then *again*. Which didn't worry me *that* much — after my kill I was as full of confidence as I was of sardines (sardines being preferable to rat parts on any intelligent kitten's menu) but enough to ensure that I wasted no time on pride and preening. Instead, I planned my next kill, just as I'd done when my mother had first died (even though I was no longer desperate for food); tried to hunt as much with forethought and intelligence as with instinct, rejigging my watches, just as the captain liked the rest of the crew to do sometimes, so that I was always extra-vigilant at those times of day when the rats were most likely to be out and about. So it was that at dusk the following evening, most of the crew having just eaten their evening meal, I was patrolling the various passageways amidships.

It was the sound that came first, and it stopped me in my tracks, streaking through my body like a bolt of electricity.

"You alright, Blackie?" said my new friend, Jack, he of the first rat encounter. Jack was the youngest of the ship's telegraphists, which meant he was in charge of communications, of which, on the *Amethyst*, there seemed to be many different kinds. He spent a lot of his time in a particularly pleasing place I'd recently discovered — the wireless office, which was situated forward, near the wheelhouse, and had a rather nice high place in it — a cosy kitten-sized nook. It was a warm wooden shelf and I had already taken quite a shine to it, both on account of its location and its proximity to various electrical items that beeped and tapped and often grew pleasingly warm as well.

Jack was at the stores today, seeing the quartermaster for a tin of herrings-in-tomato-sauce, and had obviously noticed my sudden immobility and stricken pose.

Was I alright? I realised I couldn't provide him with an answer, because I wasn't sure. Though my brain told me I was fine, other bits of me were disagreeing with it — which, as I learned early on, is often the way it works with felines; our ears and whiskers are laws unto themselves. I strained to listen, trying to believe I hadn't heard what I'd just thought I had. But since no sensible cat refuses to believe the evidence of their own ears, I was already inclining to the view that I had *indeed* heard what I thought I had, when it came again, and then again, several times in quick succession, leaving me in no doubt that my terror was well founded. It couldn't be, surely? But it was, even so. It was the sound of *barking*. There was a *dog* aboard the *Amethyst*!

Since the barking kept happening and I was still fluffed and frozen, Jack obviously worked out what had frightened me. And he laughed. (This sort of response to such troubling developments never ceased to amaze me.) "Ah," he said, "you've heard her, then? That's just our Peg. Nothing to worry about. You've got nothing to fear from her. Bark's worse than her bite, isn't it, Dusty?"

"She hasn't even *got* a bite," the man in charge of the herrings corrected him. "Not that anyone's ever noticed, anyway. Daft as a brush, that one. Wouldn't hurt a fly. Well, I say that. She might easily lick a man to death. Had a screw loose from birth, I reckon, she has."

I felt my fur settling flatter, and my pulse slow a little. Though, for all their smiles, I was by no means reassured. They seemed to talk about Peggy (a *dog*! I still couldn't believe it!) as if she posed absolutely no danger at all, and that surely couldn't be right, could it? What kind of dog was she? I mentally flipped through the dog-dossier in my head, which was, for obvious reasons, pretty flimsy. Not to mention largely half forgotten these days.

I tried to picture this Peggy, this "daft-as-a-brush" dog, this "wouldn't-hurt-a-fly" dog. This dog with "a screw loose from birth". None of these statements made sense to me, so they didn't help reassure me. Neither did any recollection I could come up with from Hong Kong. I certainly remembered seeing tiny dogs from time to time, which were usually bought, sold and kept in bamboo cages, but those dogs had a yip more like a bird's call. And they were the exception; the ones to which my mother said I need pay no mind. Every *other* dog I had ever encountered had been scary in the utmost; invariably a muscular brown whirl of aggression, growls and panting, their eyes white-tinged, their teeth dripping drool.

Having frightened myself all over again, I decided to leave them to it. From the depth of her bark, Peggy seemed *extremely* unlikely to be a tiny fluff-ball, which meant — and the thought was of scant relief, but some, at least — she was also unlikely to be able to go where I could. And since I was well-versed in the skill of evading dogs by diving into places they couldn't — high places, small places, places that could only be accessed by superior feline climbing skills — I turned tail in the passageway, left Jack to his chortlings with Dusty and headed off in the direction of a rat run I'd newly discovered, which took them beneath one of the boats stowed on the starboard side of the ship.

But it seemed Jack wasn't done with me yet. I was scooped up before I'd even managed to get out of earshot, then unceremoniously wedged under his arm. "Time you two met," he said. "Properly. Or else you'll be scrapping."

I miaowed my disapproval. I miaowed it again, louder. I miaowed it a third time, somewhat desperately

54

and shrilly, as with every step Jack took, the barking seemed to be getting louder. I was by now beside myself, wriggling furiously. What was he *thinking*? He was even whistling, which only compounded my confusion. What had possessed him? You didn't "meet" a dog. Not if you were a cat, much less a kitten. You turned tail and *ran*, for your very life!

"Oh, I *know*," Jack said soothingly. Though exactly *what* he knew he failed to share with me. "I know, feller," he said again. "But you just be gentle with our Peggy, okay?" Which confused me even more. *Me*, be gentle with *Peggy*? But trapped as I was, I remembered I was a ship's cat, and must therefore try to accept my fate — and perhaps my death — with dignity. "Try" being the operative word in this case, as I'd quite left all vestiges of dignity behind, and it was only the firmness of Jack's grip and my possibly misplaced trust in him that stopped me from disgracing myself.

We finished up in the after-mess no more than a couple of minutes later. I had previously enjoyed being with the sailors in the mess, particularly at this time of day. Though the hammocks were not yet slung, (so not yet available for snoozing purposes) it was still a cosy, companionable space, full of entertaining odours — the place where, once the meals were cleared away and everything was safely stowed, they spent most of the time when they weren't working. There were lots of men in there now — the long wooden mess tables playing host to various groups of ratings, some writing letters home, others playing cards, some lying full-length on the benches — a few asleep, others just staring into space — while others, clustered in larger groups, were doing what they often did between times: something George had explained when he'd first taken me into the mess was generally called "putting the world to rights".

The world was *not* right, however. Not presently. How could it be? I knew because of the new scent that was now invading my nostrils; which wasn't rat, wasn't human, and *definitely* wasn't anything edible — but was, in fact (and the realisation made me wince; how had I not made the connection?) a scent I had already picked up on board here and there. A scent that I'd dismissed, as it couldn't *possibly* be the one I'd thought it might be, or, if it *had* been, could be easily explained away (ships do get visitors on board from time to time, after all) as not meaning — as not *possibly* meaning what it now appeared it *did* mean — that there was a dog on board the *Amethyst*. A dog that *lived* on board the *Amethyst*. A dog called Peggy that — this last the most unbelievable of all — my human friends thought I should properly get to know!

I was so full of fear by now that I knew I couldn't be held responsible for my actions. Yet still Jack held on to me. Tightly. Then came a "woof"! Then a laugh. Then another and another. And there before me, as big and brown and horrible as I'd imagined, stood a dog — an actual dog! It barked again.

The details were a blur. Ears and teeth and whites-of-eyes and general brutal fearsomeness. So there was nothing for it. With no thought for skin or

56

cloth or, indeed, tins of herring, I struggled my hardest, and finally scrabbled my way out of Jack's grip, up his shoulder, over his head and to the highest place available. Which wasn't *nearly* high enough (it being the top end of a stowed hammock) as the she-dog called Peggy, who was still barking — "Woof! Woof! Woof! Woof!" — launched herself up on hind legs that were altogether too long for comfort, and kept on going "woof, woof, woof, woof, woof, woof, woof!", while the men, to a man, just stood and *let* her!

Well, bar Jack, who was cussing and dabbing at his face. "Ruddy *hell*, Blackie!" he complained. "Thanks a *bunch!*"

"Well, what d'you expect?" laughed a young sailor called Martin, who was standing next to him. "That he'd pop a paw out and say how d'you do? Nice to meet you? C'mon, Peg, pipe down, will you? Come away now. It's just the cat."

"He'll have her eye out, an' all," observed the one called Paddy, looking at Jack. "He's certainly got some claws on him for a little 'un," he added, inspecting the blood that was now running down Jack's face. "Quite a scram, that. Here, get him down," he said, grabbing Peggy by the thick leather collar that I belatedly realised was fastened around her neck. Which was a relief, but only briefly, because, far from reassuring me of my safety, it only seemed to endorse the fact that she was every bit as dangerous as I'd feared. Still, I was grateful. At least for the half-second before I realised that George (who'd now arrived in the after-mess as well) was intent on getting me down from my place of safety, despite the desperation with which I now hissed at him.

"You're alright," he soothed, though he wrenched me bodily off the canvas even so. And with scant regard for my claws, which were very keen to stay attached to it. "Here you go," he said, "come on, boy — you might as well get used to her. Gotta rub along, you two have, after all, haven't you? You're shipmates! And she wouldn't hurt you, honest —"

"It's not Blackie I'd be worried about," Jack pointed out, with apparent feeling. Had I not been so terrified that I thought I might pass out, I'd have had more space in my head to feel terrible about his face. As it was, though, I didn't, because I was trapped in George's hands now, and was being manoeuvred to within inches of the slobbering animal's face. Did they not *realise*? Could they not *see*? It could *eat* me in a couple of mouthfuls! Yes, I could see that it — she, whatever — was being tethered to one of my human friends by that collar of hers, but the fact that he not only held her but also straddled her with his knees didn't inspire confidence. Was she really that difficult to restrain? And if so, what were they thinking? Had the whole ship gone completely insane?

"Come on, Blackie," George was saying. "See, she's just a big old softie." For which statement there seemed to only be evidence to the contrary, because even as he said it the dog kept going "woof woof woof woof!" and her tail kept going "thwack thwack thwack thwack!" against Paddy's legs.

I drew my lips back — I had teeth too, and I wasn't afraid to use them — and though I couldn't escape George's clutches I also had claws. There was nothing for it. I pinged them forth again, shot a paw out and made a sideways swipe at the horrible animal's nose.

And, inexplicably, I was suddenly free! How had *that* happened? George must have decided to let go of me, I decided. So I hit the ground running, and I ran for my very life. As I bounded away I heard the bark change to a yowling, and Jack saying, "Well, *that* went well, didn't it?"

But it seemed Peggy hadn't followed me — or she hadn't been allowed to. That was the main thing. So perhaps they weren't going to let her get to me, after all. Just to be sure, though, I decided I'd abandon that evening's rat hunt, and hide in the safety and sanctuary of the officers' wardroom instead. At least till I had recovered from my shock and fright.

Which, bafflingly, nobody seemed to be paying any heed to. I could still hear them all laughing, even out on the upper deck.

So I was living, and I was definitely learning. I soon learned that there were two reasons why it had taken so long for me to meet Peggy — the first being that, being a dog, she tended to sleep when it was dark, like most of the humans, and — as yet, anyway — was never ordered to do any night watches. And the second was that she'd spent several days confined to "barracks", having managed to get a rusty nail wedged in her foot (I remembered my mum telling me that dogs could be prone to such mishaps) and had been made to stay safe inside while it healed.

It healed. And once that happened it became clear that there would be no means of avoiding her, despite the great pains I took over the next couple of days to ensure that I wouldn't bump into her — or that I wasn't in a position where I could be forced into a confined space and risk being made to "meet" her again.

But there would be no way around it in the longer term. That was the thing that really galled me and worried me. I would have to find some way to live with this creature, for if I couldn't, what on earth would I do? I was official "ship's cat" (a post I was proud to hold now, and which I loved) and Peggy, to my mortification, was apparently the ship's dog, and since we were aboard the *same* ship there really *wasn't* any way around it. We would both have to do what Captain Griffiths had already ordered. We would just have to learn to "rub along".

But how could that work? I spent many an hour pondering that problem. It didn't just fill me with anxiety and dread, it went against everything my mother had told me. And not only because of *what* she'd told me — *cats and dogs, kitten. No. And that's all you* need *to know* — *just stay well away from them* — but also because it had been a dog that had killed her. How could I ever forget that?

Except, *had* it? No, in truth, it had not. It had been the car that had killed her. Yes, it was true that it had been a dog who'd been chasing her, causing her to run blindly into the road — something she would never have done otherwise. But it had been the car that had actually *killed* her, so though it upset me to question my mother, I now did. I no longer had a choice in the matter, did I?

And little by little, despite the clamouring of my instincts, I began to get a sense that the fearsome Peggy she-dog might not be quite as fearsome as she'd first seemed. There were little things, for example, that didn't make sense to me, such as a couple of days later, when I was taking advantage of a sunny spot up on one of the whalers, and Petty Officer Griffiths — yes, same name as the captain — passed below me. Peggy was trotting at his side — and just getting used to *that* was hard enough in itself. But then she'd barked at me — as frantically as ever — and I'd naturally hissed down at her, and then Petty Officer Griffiths had said, with something of a note of exasperation, "Look, Simon — she just wants to be *friends* with you. See? Look at her *tail* going! She *likes* you. She *does*."

Which made me think. Her tail "going". What did that mean? Yet another thing to puzzle over. Shouldn't I be concerned about her tail "going"? If a cat's tail was moving — particularly at the frequency Peggy's seemed to — that was definitely something for a kitten to be concerned about, particularly if the cat in question was considerably bigger. Was that not so for dogs? I wished I knew.

There were also the things people said, and were still saying to me, like, "Go easy on her, Blackie" and,

"She's just a big old softie", as if (and I really couldn't fathom this at *all*) the fearsome one was actually *me*!

So I continued to observe her, and continued to ponder, and continued to make it my business to avoid her where possible, at least until I could make a bit more sense of things. I might have carried on doing so long into the future if it hadn't been for the moment which probably had to come eventually, when I rounded a corner and she rounded another and there we were, face to face, on the quarterdeck, all alone.

For once, Peggy didn't bark. Didn't blink. Didn't move. She just stood there for a second or two and stared at me. And, perhaps because she hadn't barked — as yet — I stared right back at her. And then I noticed her tail, which was wagging behind her, like a jacaranda sapling that's been caught in a stiff breeze.

Which means she likes you, I reminded myself, because that's what they'd said, hadn't they? And I kept trying to remember that, over and over, though with a marked lack of conviction. And then, quite without warning, she began walking towards me, trotting right up across the deck to me, all tongue and ears and eyeballs, and then, to my astonishment, she carried straight on past me!

I spun around. She did likewise. I spun again. She did too. And it was only after we'd danced around each other five or six times that I realised she wasn't trying to catch me, or maul me, or have me for dinner, but in fact was doing exactly what a cat would (if only to a relative) — just having a sniff, to say hello.

62

Tentatively, anxiously, I moved around to return the compliment, trying hard to resist the instinct to run away.

I made the appropriate hello back, feeling it was a rather strange thing to be doing. After all, aside from rats and humans (though I'd obviously changed my mind about the humans), dogs had always been my mortal enemy. More importantly, I had no idea how to communicate with a dog either, and wasn't quite sure where to start.

Happily, as I stood there dithering, wondering if I should continue with the sniffing, two young ratings clattered up the deck towards us, both carrying mops and buckets.

"Would you look at these two?" one said, putting his bucket down with a clang. "See? Told you they'd be fine when it came to it, didn't I?"

"Woof!" said Peggy, seeing them both. "Woof woof woof woof!"

Then she scampered back off down the deck and disappeared into a passageway.

I felt no such compulsion. In fact, quite the opposite. I sat down on the deck and began furiously washing my hindquarters. A dog. I had just been licked by a *dog*. I really didn't know *what* to think.

CHAPTER
SEVEN

The stars, when at sea, looked magnificent. They'd be magnificent anywhere, because stars can't help but sparkle, but when viewed from the ocean, many miles away from the land, they have a brightness and depth and complexity and beauty that is beyond anything that exists on the earth.

They were also a constant — a reminder that no matter how far I travelled, I could look up and see the same sky above me as I had as a kitten in Hong Kong. And it was comforting to think that, no matter where my new life as a ship's cat might now take me, my mother could — and, I hoped, did — still watch over me.

On board ship, though, every aspect of my life was now different — so much so that I sometimes had to stop and take stock of quite how much it had changed since the day George had smuggled me aboard.

For starters, I was living on the sea rather than the land, which was a very strange business for a cat, not least because my mother had been quite right about water, and how much I disliked being "wet through". Curiously, though, it was a much drier world than the one I'd left on dry land. Yes, there were times when it was necessary to keep away from mops and buckets, but there was never any issue of having to hunt in teeming rain, to leap puddles, or to pad through muddy gloop.

Neither did I now have to defend my "territory" — something I'd only just begun to understand as a concept when George had taken me from the harbour, and one that, as a young kitten, had always loomed rather threateningly. Having a territory might be necessary, but there was nothing nice about it, as it seemed mostly to comprise a non-stop round of boundary-patrolling, invariably involving lots of angry confrontations, facing up to cats with bigger expansion plans than I had.

But all that — to my great joy — was a thing of the past now. Here there would be no such confrontations to have to deal with. Well, bar perhaps the odd one with Peggy. But as it had quickly become obvious that Peggy's idea of "confrontation" was to greet you as if she loved you more than anything in the world, the only worry there was the foulness of her well-meaning tongue, dogs not being so particular as cats in matters of personal hygiene.

Though I did, I supposed, still have a kind of territory to patrol. No longer one of trees, sand and blossoms, and things that roosted, cawed and crawled, but one of steel and salty spray, enamel, oil and engines, of machines and the materials of men. A territory of ladders, too, which I had finally found the means to negotiate, and which had turned out to be not quite so terrifying as I'd supposed. No, it wasn't easy to go *down* a ladder, and at first I'd made laborious diversions to avoid doing so. But when there was no option but to descend one, I had no choice but to be courageous and, bit by bit — to my great delight — I managed to conquer my fear.

Moreover, it was a territory I found myself sharing very willingly — an occurrence that never ceased to amaze me, not least because of how natural it had quickly come to feel. Should it have? On this point I was still very baffled, because adult cats (as far as I knew) shunned company and lived alone, and that was supposedly the way they preferred it.

Yet here I was sharing my territory, very happily, with some one hundred and seventy humans and a dog, name of Peggy. A *dog*. A real, living, breathing, *actual* dog. Sometimes I'd wake up from a nap in the captain's cap, then see or hear Peggy, and think I must surely still be dreaming.

Most pleasing and surprising was how much I loved my human family, and no less was the revelation of how much they seemed to love me too.

Yes, I'd come on board with George, but he'd laid no particular claim to me, clear from the outset that I (together with the good luck I would apparently confer on their endeavours) was to be there for them all. Though I reported to Captain Griffiths, I *was* very much there for everyone, and though they couldn't possibly know just how much I understood of them (that human thing again) it quickly seemed I had another role to play aboard the *Amethyst* — to be the official recipient of sailors' secrets.

Whether I was in one of the officers' cabins, or somewhere in the packed after-mess, every sailor seemed to have things in his head that he kept to himself. So it was that my role began not just as a rat catcher, but as a confidant as well, hearing all about the things they seemed to find it difficult to share with one another — the same sorts of things, in the main, that I would share with the moon when sitting on the end of my jetty. I heard about crushes and sweethearts, fiancées and wives. About their families, about the children and animals whose images danced across various bulkheads; about the babies a few of my friends had apparently fathered, but, heart-breakingly, had yet to even meet. I heard of memories and musings, regrets and resolutions, recriminations, and sometimes, when days at sea became rain-sodden and endless, it was my job to curl up close while one of my friends had a cry, which was sometimes upsetting for them, but at other times, also a blessing. "You're a good listener, Blackie," they'd whisper, furiously drying their eyes. "And I know you'll keep mum."

Keeping "mum", I soon learned, was a very important thing. And having responsibility for keeping it (and the men's faith that I could be trusted to, of course) always made me feel close to my own mother.

None of this was a part of my mother's plan for me, however. Far from it. I'd catch myself (as likely when cuddled up in a sleeping sailor's hammock as when presenting a lifeless rat to the captain) in a state of bemused wonder. Specially at those times when the stars were at their brightest — at three or four or five in the morning, perhaps while I was sitting on some sheltered part of the upper deck, watching flying fish skim the water, perhaps sitting in the humming warmth of the wireless room, perhaps curled up on my favourite spot up on the bridge. I'd be sitting companionably with the captain, or Lieutenant Weston (or even Lieutenant Berger, however much he kept declaring himself not to be "a cat person") and wishing so hard that my mother could see for herself that humans — at least the ones on His Majesty's Ship *Amethyst* — were not the monsters she'd supposed.

It was the strangest thing — I had gone from being an outsider, a loner, a scared, scavenging kitten, to being a valued member of a team. No longer hiding in the shadows, for fear of being seen and mistreated, here I was treated daily to titbits and cuddles and strokes. It made no sense, because these were not things a cat should desire, yet at the same time I had never felt so happy. And as the days turned into weeks, and the weeks into months, I realised that solitude was not only overrated, it was the least likely thing I'd be now inclined to choose, with a human lap the most likely, any day.

There was a great deal to learn about life in the Navy, and I was eager to learn it. Not least (as it was key to almost everything on board) the many ways my human friends communicated with one another, which was something they seemed to like to do almost all the time, even more so — and this was a revelation too —

than the ever barking, ever sniffing, ever tail-wagging Peggy.

Yes, they spoke to each other, of course, and for the most part, that was easy to grasp. Had Captain Griffiths been a cat, the *Amethyst* would very much be his territory, though, unlike a cat, he didn't need to defend it alone; he had all his men, who deferred to him at all times and in all things, to assist him in doing it.

Then there were things called flags, of which there seemed to be many; not just the ensign that flew from the top of that masthead to let everyone know who we were. There was a big store of flags below, each in its own designated cubby hole, all of them made of a mix of different coloured cloths, all of them enticing to a cat in want of a nap. Though I learned very quickly that a cat in want of a nap might — no, *would* — do much better to take it elsewhere, because (as the signals officer was at great pains to relay when he ejected me) no one interfered with his bunting. I wasn't sure what he meant by "bunting" but, as ever, his tone was very clear; that everything to do with flags — hoisting them, flying them and then bringing them down again and refolding them — was taken very seriously indeed.

Closer to home, there were myriad different ways by which everyone communicated on board. As well as everyone being called different things by different people (which was why I'd been gifted two names, I supposed) there was a big noisy bell, which was rung periodically, as well as a bewildering number of different whistles, which were blown in so many ways, and for so many apparent reasons, that I never knew if there was going to be a sudden invasion of mops and buckets or a very important person coming aboard.

Most curious of all, though, were the serpentine devices that wound their way around the *Amethyst* and, by some magic that I had yet to understand (and perhaps never would), enabled everyone to speak to whoever they wished to speak to, in whichever compartment of the ship they happened to be.

They were strange things — a little too unnervingly snakelike, to my mind — but without doubt, very clever indeed: lidded metal tubes that began in one place — say, the bridge — and ended up somewhere else — say the wireless room or wheelhouse — carrying words wherever words needed to be.

"That's called a voice pipe," the captain told me, when I was up on the bridge with him one morning, sitting on the ship's compass (which being glass-topped, was always nice to sit on when the sun happened to be shining, though best avoided if there was a nip in the air). The pipe was adjacent, and I was busy making a closer inspection of it. "And, let me tell you, young fellow, if you let your curiosity get the better of you and decide to see where it might take you, you'll be in for an *extremely* rude awakening." He'd laughed then. "And probably get stuck fast then, as well, even being the little tiddler you are."

I had no idea what a rude awakening might feel like, but I was definitely more than familiar with being "stuck", having never forgotten being stuck up a tree. It was sufficient to deter me from investigating them any further.

Most fascinating of all, though, were the machines that went tap-tap-tap-tap and lived in the wireless room. It was a place that had quickly become a favourite haunt for me anyway — what with all the paper lying around ("very important bits of paper!" Jack would huff, every time he shifted me off from them) — it had lots of very cat-friendly features. But the machines were particularly interesting. They didn't look much, but could apparently send important messages all around the world, just by the operator (of which Jack was one) tapping bits of wood against one another.

There was something mesmeric about the tap-tap machines, so much so that I'd spend long periods dozing beside the telegraphists — Jack in particular. This had initially been because his preferred snack was a herring sandwich, but latterly just because, well, because Jack was Jack, and there was so much with Jack that was tacitly understood. I sometimes wondered if Jack could tell what I was thinking.

I could see him doing it, despite the fact that the main thing about the tap-taps was their ability to put me, if not quite to sleep, in that delicious drowsy half-sleep that cats like the best; my "meditations on the mouse", as George once had put it.

"Shall I tell you what this is?" Jack explained to me. "This here is what's known as a code machine. Named after a chap called Samuel Morse — since you obviously want to know that — who was something of a clever man, and who helped devise a way of communicating using pulses of electricity, and that's really all you need to know."

He was wrong about that — ideally I'd have liked to know everything about everything — but I was happy enough, for now anyway, just to understand the principle. And once again to discover that humans, working together, were so much more the sum of all their parts, all of them contributing in different ways to achieving the amazing variety of things humans seemed to want to do.

But I had another thing to learn in those early months on board the *Amethyst*. That just when you are growing content, thinking everything is exactly as you like it, life has a way of seeing to it that you get something else.

Change was a normal part of life in the Navy; I had quickly learned that. You followed your orders and went wherever you were told. As did the *Amethyst*. We sailed and we docked and we oiled and replaced supplies, and by the end of the year we had travelled all over the ocean — and also up a river; the mighty Yangtse, to Nanking.

But, as well as that, people came and people went. First George, gentle George, who I would be forever grateful to, and who was posted off to another ship that autumn.

And there were others, some I'd known, some I'd barely got to know yet — off to different postings, new adventures, exciting places. And in their stead would come new sailors, often pink-cheeked and so innocent-looking they barely seemed men yet, their kit sharp and clean and their caps fresh from their boxes — they were called "boy-sailors", and very aptly so.

But by far the biggest change — and the most upsetting personally, was the news that Lieutenant Commander Griffiths was leaving us. I found out quite by chance, too, when I wandered into his cabin just before we were about dock in Hong Kong one day, and came upon him packing up his things.

Being now so much a sea cat (or salty sea dog, which the captain had once called me, rather confusingly) I tended to make myself scarce whenever the *Amethyst* docked. Once we were alongside a wharf, I had quickly learned, there would be a period of noisy mayhem — people flooding aboard, stores being loaded and unloaded, sailors to-ing and fro-ing and generally being busy, in that way that was peculiar to being in a port. It was the part of the ship's routine that, though still routine, never felt so to me. Quite the opposite.

Unlike Peggy, who seemed to revel in the fuss strangers made of her, I preferred to nap my way through the chaos, only emerging back on deck when I could hear the reassuring throb of the boilers making steam again. Who knew what might happen when in port, after all? Just as George had taken me from the dock to start my new life, who was to say that someone might not just snatch me off the *Amethyst* and take me right back again? Or, less dramatically, but also more feasibly, that I'd accidentally curl up in something that was destined to be returned to land? A basket of laundry, perhaps. Or a trunk. Or some box or crate or bundle. It *could* happen. No, not likely, but I never ruled it out. I didn't dare to, because I'd dreamed about it once. About the stomach-churning business of waking up, confused, and seeing my home moving away from me; my dear *Amethyst*, steaming into the distance, getting smaller and smaller . . .

It was silly — *so* silly — but the feeling never really left me. And I didn't think it ever would. At sea I was happy. On land I had not been. Not since I'd found myself alone and so afraid. I couldn't imagine living on land ever again.

Glad as I was to reach the captain's cabin and escape the mayhem, once inside, there it struck me anew. My beloved captain, who I couldn't quite believe was leaving us — leaving *me* — was looking just as he always did when the *Amethyst* came into port. He was as smart and shiny as the pins the men furiously polished, and as straight and tall as the *Amethyst's* mast. As was the custom when entering port, he had dressed for the occasion and was an even more shipshape and Bristol fashion version of his normal self.

He smiled when he saw me, and I wished, as I did sometimes, that I could find a way to have him tell me what Bristol fashion did mean. I wondered if I'd ever find out now. "Well, well, come on in, my little friend," he said, patting the bed covers on his bunk. "Come to say goodbye, have you? Bless you. I'm going to miss you."

He reached down to stroke me, in his usual firm, no-non-sense fashion. I knew he dared not pick me up, though. My white fur had a habit of shedding when he was dressed in his dark clothes; even more so than the black did when he was decked out in his whites. So I sprang up onto the bed so I could at least be close beside him while he gathered together the last of his things. Sadness came over me. I knew I would miss him terribly.

"You know what, Simon?" he said, reaching out to slide a hand down my back again. "For two pins, I'd pop you into my trunk and take you home with me, you know that?"

I purred as loudly as I could so he would know I understood. I'd have also liked to let him know that a part of me would like that too, even as I was in no doubt that my home now was here. How would they cope with the rats without me? Who would the men confide their secrets to? How would Jack manage without me when he was all alone at night doing his watch, with only his Morse code machine to keep him company?

But I think the captain knew that too. He continued to stroke me, staring out into space for some time, before starting to pick carefully at the sticky tape at the corners of the small collection of photographs that were clustered above his bed. From the captain to the Chinese mess boys — it seemed to make no difference. Everyone on board seemed to have a collection such as this: pictures of people and places they missed. And, in the captain's case, of several cats, too. I wondered where they were now — what might have become of them. "That's the thing with cats," he said eventually, perhaps reading my mind. "You're so supremely adaptable, you felines. Fit yourselves in just about anywhere. Plop you down wherever and you just get on with it, don't you?"

I thought about how little my mother would have expected that I'd be living anywhere other than Stonecutters Island, and decided he was probably right. I had always imagined I would too. Yet here I was.

He rubbed the little cleft beneath my mouth, and then smiled at one of the photographs, which was of two little girls, sitting in an armchair. He put it down on the bed beside me, and started on another. This one was a boy, who I thought must be his son. How did he feel to know they were so far away? "And this here," he then said, "is Peter Puss." He placed another picture on the pile, of him standing in uniform with a cat draped over his shoulder. "He's a she," he went on. Then he grinned. "I know. Confusing, isn't it? Ship's cat on the *Brissenden*, while I was serving as lieutenant. Just after the war ended, that was. Feels like a long time ago now . . . Anyway, I'm sure you don't want to hear about *that*." He tapped the picture. "Now *there's* a cat and a half for you, Simon — she even had a litter of kittens while on active duty. How about that?"

He added a couple more pictures to the pile. "You know, us sailors aren't that different to you cats, really, are we?" he mused. "We go where we're posted, we fit in and get on with it. Just like Peter Puss here. We do our best. That's the naval way, you see."

Captain Griffiths had been in the Navy for a long time. He'd fought in the war. He'd captained a famous ship called the *Riou*. He'd been courageous, and for his bravery the Navy had given him several medals. He had done his best. He was clearly a fine captain indeed.

But, to me, he was a man who'd been kind, and I would miss him, and I worried about the new captain who was coming to take his place. Would he like me? Would I like him? Would he give me a "roving commission" too? Would he want me to accompany him on his rounds?

There was no way of knowing, and not much I could do about it, either, so I'd just have to do what Captain Griffiths said — get on with it. And it wouldn't be long now, anyway; I could feel that the engines were slowing. We'd soon be docking in Hong Kong. And soon after that, I'd find out.

He was nearly ready. The small pile of photographs was almost complete, but for one picture that he was removing from the bulkhead particularly carefully. It was clearly old, and I had a hunch it had been stuck up on many a ship before this one. He finally freed it, and placed it down on the pile with the others, before seeming to reconsider. He picked it up again.

"I never did tell you, did I?" he mused, tapping a finger to my nose. Then he smiled a strange smile and lifted the picture closer to his face. He touched it lightly with the same finger, and then nodded towards me. "You know who that is, Simon?" he said, holding it out

77

again, for me to look at. It was of a young, beautiful lady (the "darling wife" he sometimes spoke of? Or some other person? Perhaps his mother?) and cradled in her arms was a bundle wrapped in a shawl. It was a baby. I knew because I'd seen lots of pictures of babies now — even a couple their young fathers had yet to meet. "That's your namesake, that is," said Captain Griffiths. "That's Simon."

He didn't say any more, but he didn't need to. I'd been with humans now for long enough to understand them so much better. So I knew; I knew immediately, from the way he said the words to me, and from the way he quickly cast his eyes heavenwards as he spoke. That the Simon in the photograph was gone.

And I realised that the distance between cats and humans wasn't so great. Whoever *that* Simon was — and perhaps that didn't even matter — he was up with my mother, among the stars.

CHAPTER
EIGHT

The period immediately after Captain Griffiths left us had been a strange one.

The new captain joined the ship — he was called Lieutenant Commander Bernard Skinner, and he had such a round, smooth and gentle-looking face that I wondered if he'd been one of the boy-sailors in the war — this war that meant nothing to me, but that everyone still seemed to talk about. But though he scarcely looked old enough to command a whole ship, there was something in his manner that seemed to suggest otherwise, something in the way he held himself that put me in mind of some of the cats back on Stonecutters whose territory abutted mine. His was a presence that commanded respect.

I knew it would be some time before we properly got to know each other, but there was good news right away. The first lieutenant assured me that he was a cat lover like Captain Griffiths, which meant my position was probably safe up on the bridge. I hated the idea of giving up my spot on the magnetic compass — not to mention the other spot I enjoyed, in hazy weather: the little box-on-the-wall at the back of the bridge which housed lots of important wires. But I was still keen to make a good impression on the new commander, and immediately set about hunting down a rat to present to him, so he would know I was a cat who pulled my weight.

And there was another change afoot, it seemed. A big one. Within days of Captain Skinner joining us, we celebrated something called Christmas, which was entirely new to me; an odd business that seemed to involve all sorts of peculiar rituals, few of which made a great deal of sense to me (setting fire to your pudding?) and some of which, particularly the things they had appropriately called "crackers", weren't nice at all. They were terrifying.

Happily, it didn't last long and, as far as I could tell, the men were rather glad of it all being over, too. After all, though it inspired lots of singing, and a bumper load of extra post when we'd docked at Shanghai, it also inspired a surprising degree of sadness among some of the crew, and, on one unfortunate occasion, following extra rum rations, a leading seaman getting punched on the nose.

But such was the "mystery of the human condition" — a phrase I'd picked up from Captain Griffiths — that, once the "festivities" were done with (along with another bout of bizarre behaviour, to do with "seeing in" the new year, apparently) a collective glumness seemed to settle over the *Amethyst*, like the sooty spewings of a badly maintained engine.

The rats, in contrast, seemed to be full of the joys of the coming spring; they certainly sprung away with gusto almost every time I got near one, driving me almost to distraction.

So it was that I met Captain Skinner before being able to dispatch one to present to him. Instead, I met him quite by accident, a good couple of weeks after he'd assumed command, while keeping Jack company in the wireless room, as usual.

I was taking my rest on some of his Very Important Bits of Paper when the captain appeared, snapping me out of my reverie (about some very important rat-related matters) and making Jack, who had his back to him, jump.

"Ah, the ship's cat!" he boomed, coming in on a cloud of some exotic spicy odour — one that I was fairly sure had not been present on the *Amethyst* up to now.

He picked me up without further ado (this was clearly the way with captains) setting both my whiskers and nostrils into overdrive all at once.

"He's called Simon, sir," Jack told him. "Well, Blackie, more often than not, sir. One of the ratings found him back last May, sir, on Stonecutters Island. Ordinary Seaman Hickinbottom. Left the ship before Christmas. Mangy little stray, he was. Probably orphaned. Just a kitten then. Nothing of him. Didn't think he were more than a few months old when he found him. Erm, sir."

Just as Captain Griffiths had, Captain Skinner now held me at arm's length for inspection. He had one hand round my tummy, so my front legs dangled over the back of his hand, and the other thoughtfully cupped under my hindquarters. It wasn't the most dignified position a cat could find itself in, but I'd grown used to the idea that a naval cat needed to be understanding in such situations. I couldn't expect the captain of one of His Majesty's frigates to get down on his hands and knees, after all.

The new captain chortled, revealing a row of cheerful teeth. "There's not a great deal of him *now*!" he told Jack, as if giving him an order to rethink. "Still quite the tiddler, aren't you, boy?"

"But he's an excellent ratter, sir," Jack was quick to reassure him.

"Often the way," the captain mused. "He'll be lighter on his feet." He brought me back closer to his face then, and I could see he had eyes almost the same colour as my mother had. Warm eyes, like berries. He then put me back down on Jack's pull-down Morse code machine desk. "As you were, old chap," he said to me. "So now, Signals, what have you got for me?" and began looking through some of the piles of Very Important Bits of Paper, and various scribbled notes Jack routinely had at his side. And as I settled down to a decent grooming — mangy stray, indeed! — I remembered what Jack had said about "when" I was still a kitten. So I'd been right, then. I'd officially left my kittenhood behind. I was a grown cat not just in my own eyes, but in their eyes as well. I stretched a little taller. Actually *felt* a little taller. Because it was quite a milestone, that. I was a cat now. It was official.

I couldn't help thinking about what my mother had told me about bad luck, and kittens, and cages. I supposed I was now grown enough for that protection to be behind me, which made me even more glad (as if I could have been any gladder) to have been chosen to live the seafaring life.

For there were no men who put cats in cages living here. On board the *Amethyst* I was free, and I was safe.

And I was safe, and also free, for a long time. We all were. And Captain Skinner turned out to be much like Captain Griffiths — stern when he needed to be, soft when he didn't, and as appreciative of a dead rat as the next man. Well, assuming the next man was a naval man, anyway.

Captain Skinner was also happy to have a ship's cat among the company. Though he didn't whistle for me (and it would be impolite to follow him around without permission), he seemed very happy to have me in the wardroom during meal times, particularly when we had visiting naval dignitaries on board, where he liked most for me to entertain them.

But a ship at sea, previously a warship, as the *Amethyst* had been, was not always about entertaining visiting dignitaries. Her new role — and her white post-war livery reflected it well — was always to try to help keep the peace.

So when we were given our orders, midway through April 1949, it was odd to begin hearing whispers around the ship that the peace might not be as robust as everyone thought.

Though our orders were, to be fair, perfectly ordinary. Having recently spent a while in Shanghai, and had some fifteen young ratings join us, we were now being sent to relieve our sister ship, HMS *Consort*, which was stationed in Nanking to provide protection for local British residents, and in particular, the staff of the British Embassy. We were also there to bring supplies to the British and Commonwealth residents and, should they require it (which they apparently might, given China was currently such an unstable country) evacuate any nationals.

We knew Nanking, because the *Amethyst* had already done a spell of this back in December, the guardships being in place there on rotation. It had been a deployment that had gone without incident. Rather too much without incident, the way I remembered it; the crew that had been there complaining bitterly (we had been moored there for a month) that as protocol dictated they were unable to enter the city itself, they'd spent most of the time fed up, too hot, and bored witless.

Not so, Peggy and I. Peggy because she was largely witless already, and, if strapped for entertainment, would simply chase her own tail. As for me, the word "bored" took a great deal of fathoming, since it was completely beyond my comprehension. You were either busy (killing rats, tormenting cockroaches, eating, playing and so on) or you were dozing (always a pleasure), or you were asleep. So the business of being "bored" (and its sister complaint of "getting down in the dumps") was a concept I found hard to understand.

84

"Aww, Blackie," Jack would often say to me, wistfully, "oh, to be a cat, eh? Oh, to have a cat's life!" Then he'd sigh theatrically, as if somehow jealous.

But this time around, it seemed my friends might not be bored. Because though the *Amethyst* had nothing to do with the Chinese Civil War, she was still about to be pitched into the middle of it. Yes, this had been the case last time and, yes, it was true no harm had come to us, but since that time the Chinese war had begun to intensify, and all the talk in the wardroom that night was of worries that now we might be in the wrong place at the wrong time.

The concern lay in the fact that we weren't even supposed to be there: we were standing in for another ship, the Australian HMAS *Shoalhaven*. The *Shoalhaven* had already been in Shanghai, all set to go to Nanking, when the "powers that be", as Captain Skinner put it (and he'd seemed none too pleased about it, either), had changed their minds about the ship being deployed at that point, deciding that, with Anzac Day imminent (a day when Australia remembered her war dead) they were not prepared to send an Australian vessel up the Yangtse, and run the risk of their sailors being put in danger.

"So that's where we come in," Captain Skinner had explained to the crew the night before we sailed, confirming what was already being rumoured by the officers. That, with the war reaching crisis point, this trip to Nanking could, in theory, put the *Amethyst* in the line of fire instead.

Though the nationalists and communists had been at war with each other since the 1920s, a point had been reached where the communists controlled the north shore of the Yangtse river, and, though a temporary truce was apparently in place, they had made it known that if the nationalists didn't allow them to pass freely, they would make an assault on the south bank.

In just three days from now.

If I knew nothing of boredom, I knew even less of war. My only experience of human conflict was the occasional rumpus over something or other down at Stonecutters dockyard — which was usually resolved with no more than angry words being exchanged or, at the worst, someone's cart being upturned.

All I really understood about "war" — that human preoccupation that continued to confound me — was that, as far as we were concerned, it was history. War was over now — everyone always seemed to say that. We'd just had the "war to end all wars", and the older sailors on the *Amethyst* would tell the younger ones about it constantly.

"Back during the *war* . . ." they'd say, before regaling them with some spine-tingling anecdote or other. "Back when bloody Jerry had the upper hand, or so *they* thought . . ." they'd begin, before painting pictures that had the boy seamen's eyes bulging out as if on stalks. "You're lucky, lads, not to have *been* through it . . ." they'd remind them, their expressions stony, before slapping them on the backs and laughing long and loud. But for all that, it was still laughter that held enough of a note of relief to make it clear that being in a war was not a good thing.

Now war was done with, and everyone was happier as a result of it. All the talk, always, was of "keeping the peace". That was what the *Amethyst* was there for. To keep the peace. Our job was to patrol the waters around the countries of the Far East, so that no one could be in doubt that — where His Majesty's Navy was concerned, anyway — that was the way it was going to stay.

The jacarandas were in bloom in Shanghai as we left it. Blossom was everywhere — the whole hillside was dotted with colour — but it was the jacaranda blossom that most grabbed my attention, because it took me back to my kittenhood, to the same luminous purple that I remembered from when I'd left. So had it been a year? A full year since I'd gone to sea?

I decided it must have been, because I was in no doubt that the sea felt like home now; by my reckoning it had been home for longer than it had not. So as we slipped that day, smoothly and without ceremony, for Nanking, it was only the usual excitement that I felt. It was another day, another journey, another sea-going adventure. If my friends *were* bored, I would do my best to entertain them. To jolly them out of their dissatisfaction.

Little did I know that the truce that the "powers that be" had banked on was not going to hold for as long as they'd thought. And as a consequence, though we couldn't know it, for those of us aboard the *Amethyst*, the peace would soon be over as well.

PART TWO

PART TWO

CHAPTER
NINE

Yangtse River, near the village of San-Chiang-ying
08:00 hours, 20 April 1949

Animals have a way of sensing things, often long before humans. All animals can do this, because we have to rely so much on instinct — even creatures as apparently without wits as Peggy. Who knew why my own instinct was so strong that morning? But it was. I just had that feeling that something was going to happen. That all the mutterings I'd heard might have some substance after all.

But what might happen to us if they did? I didn't know. Just as I'd never known war, I had never witnessed the extremes of violence that I'd often heard about during my time aboard the *Amethyst*. Not that I hadn't seen violence happen. The death of my mother had definitely been an act of extreme violence, even though it had been an accident. I'd also known the kind of violence that was an everyday part of nature; the necessary skirmishes I'd seen animals engage in to protect their territory. But not killing. Never killing. Not the kind of slaughter I'd heard the crew talking about down in the mess. Not killing when you didn't need to eat.

But I knew such violence and intent to kill existed. How could I miss it when the evidence was all around me? After all, the *Amethyst* had been originally built as a warship, as the captain had often reminded me. And with all her guns, it would be difficult to see her as anything else. But, for all the battle drills and the regular rounds of maintenance and inspection of her armaments, I had never known her as anything other than a home. So on the morning we set off from Shanghai, bound for the city of Nanking again, the only war I'd known was the one it was my personal duty to wage — the one against the rats that were still my mortal enemy.

My only enemy, in fact. Until now.

We'd weighed anchor at 05:15 hours, under a yellowish dawn sky, only to be forced by fog to drop the anchor again. I remembered the fog that could lie on the Yangtse from the last time we'd travelled up there — a dense, opaque whiteness that would roll out across the river like a blanket. But this fog was different. You didn't so much see it as have it envelop you, damp and cool and pungent. As the Yangtse was notoriously dangerous to navigate in poor visibility, the captain had decided to stop and wait it out.

Ever mindful of both my mother and Jack's words (on one thing they were agreed — never pass up the opportunity to take a nap) I'd then taken myself off for a sleep down in the galley, which was always a good choice when the dawn was breaking, both for the warmth of the ovens (always nice after a rat hunt) and the cook, who'd be busy preparing the crew's breakfast, which inevitably meant there was a good chance of being given a scrap of bacon. I'd been fast asleep, too, it having been a long night and a busy one, what with all the strange comings and goings in the officers' wardroom and the many signals Jack was sending back and forth to Shanghai.

Most telling was that Captain Skinner seemed to be taking the threat seriously. No, this wasn't *our* war — I'd heard that said enough times that I could be in no doubt of it — but as we were going to be in what was agreed to be a potential war zone, he had already taken precautions. As soon as we'd slipped our mooring at Shanghai, headed towards Woosung and the Yangtse, he'd ordered a detail of ordinary seamen to stitch together several tarpaulins, in order to make two enormous flags. These they then painted in a precise pattern of red, white and blue, to match the Union Jack that had already been painted on the quarterdeck.

The new flags, not quite dry, were then rolled up over oars taken from the whalers, and fixed from the guardrails with sailmaker's twine — both ready to be unfurled again at a moment's notice, so that no one could be in any doubt that the *Amethyst* was a British ship, going about its lawful business for the Royal Navy.

My first real taste of war came without warning. And I must have slept deeply, because I was not so much nudged into wakefulness as pitched headlong into it, by the sound of instructions echoing round and round the voice pipes — by orders being relayed with an urgency I'd never heard before; by the furious ringing of the bell that had only one meaning: that the crew were being mustered to their action stations.

Wide awake now, I lifted my nose to see what I could get wind of on the air, but it was the captain's tone of voice that told me most. Something had happened. Or was about to. Something bad. I could sense it. I stretched long and hard and jumped down from the stove side. While the cook ran off to where he was supposed to be manning a fire hose, I hurried back up to the bridge to see what was going on.

The passageways were busy, everyone rushing to be somewhere, looking preoccupied and tense, and I could almost taste the fear that seemed to travel with them. Keeping close to the bulkheads, and out of the way of running feet, I padded quickly along my usual, now long-familiar route, feeling the same peculiar mixture of excitement and anxiety that had accompanied me on that other journey, almost a full year ago now, when I'd been tucked safely out of sight inside George's tunic. That sometimes felt as if it was a lifetime ago.

In some ways, it really *was* a lifetime ago, as I'd now been on the *Amethyst* for longer than I'd lived in Hong Kong, and, apart from when my mother visited me in snatches of strange, wistful dreams, the memories of that time were fast fading. I'd finally got my "sea legs", just as George had always told me I would, and was now, nose to tail-tip, a sailor. Which no doubt meant I now had something of a sailor's intuition to go with my animal instinct, because there was definitely a quiver in my whiskers; a sense that testing times might well lie ahead.

Though the fog had now cleared, the morning sky still looked bruised when I emerged out onto the deck, and I wondered if more might be on the way. But not as much as I wondered what other dangers lay in front of us — ones not of nature's, but of human design.

I padded across the quarterdeck, feeling the dewy dampness on the freshly painted corticene beneath my paws, and thought the time might have come to deploy the Union Jack flags. And no sooner had I taken up my usual post on the electrical box at the rear of the bridge than all the reassurance we'd hung on to of being a neutral party was blown out of the water at a stroke.

Though I'd not experienced war, I *had* known the sort of terror that grips you when you know someone or something means you harm. Someone meant to harm us now. I just sensed it.

The attack, when it came, though, seemed completely out of the blue. One minute the captain was relaying directions to the wheelhouse via the voice pipe, the next, there was a flash of flame on the shore, followed by a terrible screeching wail, and it was as if the river we'd been previously gliding along was boiling, exploding, rising — up, up, up, up! — before my eyes, in great fountains of hissing, rushing water.

Both the captain and the first lieutenant grabbed their binoculars and raised them, scanning the place from which the eruption of water might have come.

"Watch for the flashes on the bank!" barked the captain.

Though the fog had gone, the shore was still distant and murky — a hazy and indistinct bluey grey. And as I watched, another flash came, and another wall of white water exploded, this time so close it almost showered us all. I felt my claws scrabbling for purchase and my heart starting to pound, and wondered if I was about to use up every one of my lives all at once — wondering if we *all* were; feeling terrified, *terrified*, for my friends. I hadn't felt such fear since the day I had watched my mother die, and had never expected to again. I had never experienced shell fire, or anything remotely like it, and the sight and sound — the terrifying *nearness* of the explosions — came as such a shock that all my fur stood on end. And it seemed they weren't done with us yet. As I struggled to keep my balance, further licks of flame bloomed on the north bank, and more fountains of water streaked skyward.

Captain Skinner lowered his binoculars, his face set and watchful. Then he leaned into the voice pipe that snaked down below. "Bridge to wheelhouse," he barked. "Increase speed to 15 knots!" I could hear men all over the ship still hurrying to their various action stations. "Number One," he said to Weston. "See if you can get that bearing."

Thankfully, the firing ceased almost as soon as it started, and the whole thing was over in a matter of moments. And as I quivered behind Captain Skinner, wondering quite what had just happened, I was reassured to hear his voice take on a less anxious tone.

"Looks like we've just been caught in the crossfire," he said to Weston. "That salvo clearly wasn't meant for us, or they would have hit us, wouldn't they? Perhaps it was just a show of strength."

"Or they didn't see the ensign," Weston suggested.

"Maybe so." He paused and peered across at the north bank, which clearly told him little. "Well, unless we've an errant communist shore battery on our hands. Order the X gun crew to unfurl the Union Jacks just to be on the safe side." The first lieutenant did so. "In any event," he mused, scanning the north shore once again through his binoculars, "we're sitting ducks and need to be clear of this as soon as possible." He leaned again to the voice pipe. "Bridge to wheelhouse. Let's have 19 knots now. Full ahead."

He turned to me then. "You still here, Simon? Looks like you're finally seeing a bit of action, eh?" He stroked me absently. "Let's hope we don't see any more, eh?"

It was a wish that was not to be granted.

We continued up the river for several minutes, everyone on the bridge tense and watchful. Despite Captain Skinner's apparent confidence that the shells hadn't been meant for us, there was still a sense of nervous anticipation in the air. He'd been right. Whoever they'd been meant for — the nationalists on the south bank, presumably — we were right in the path of any further fire directed their way.

The minutes continued to pass, though, and with every mile we put between ourselves and whoever had fired on us, I began to feel a little less frightened. We'd soon be clear of the wayward battery and could relax, if only a little. Even so, my hackles kept rising and I refused to be reassured, and, ever conscious that the captain might need to take decisive action, I decided to go below again and get out of his way.

I jumped down from my box, and made my way down the ladder to the foredeck, passing Frank, who was hurrying up it past me, his eyes focused up and forward. He almost vaulted me, seemingly oblivious to my being there.

Other than that, I saw no one. The whole crew were on alert still, everyone manning their various stations. From the passageway that led to the captain's cabin, which seemed as sensible a place to go as any, the thing I could feel, over and above everything else, was the vibration under my paws as the huge turbines toiled beneath me; powering the *Amethyst* at a speed I had yet to feel her go, and churning the water into an angry, boiling soup.

But it seemed there was more than one shore battery keeping watch on our progress, because no sooner had I hopped up onto the captain's desk, in order to see out of the scuttle, than the *Amethyst* lurched violently to starboard, knocking me off my feet. I scrabbled back up, but no sooner had I got my balance once again than another blast — another *shell!* — made the water foam in front of me. Just as I recognised that I should immediately take cover, I was ripped from my feet again, the air torn from my lungs, and the world swam away from me and disappeared.

CHAPTER
TEN

When I woke I could hear nothing but the drone of a mosquito. For a time I simply focused on the low, monotone buzzing sound, and tried to work out where I was. I was lying on a bunk, so my first thought was that I was still in Captain Skinner's cabin, but something felt wrong. I struggled to clear my head enough to work out what it was. I was definitely in a cabin, but which? Not the captain's. I couldn't be in the captain's, because . . . because . . . because *what*? Try as I might, I couldn't seem to focus. I looked around me, sideways on, only one eye fully open, and at last my gaze came to rest on something that looked familiar — the collection of photographs pinned on the bulkhead opposite, which I recognised as belonging to Petty Officer Griffiths. I saw his locker then, as well. The place where he often parked his cap. But there was no cap. It was now open, the lid upright and some of the clothing spewing out of it, as if caught in the act of escaping.

I strained to listen; to pick up something other than the mosquito's incessant whining, and realised that it wasn't even a mosquito — the noise was a constant ringing inside my ears. But there was nothing to help me make sense of what had happened. I hadn't the slightest idea of how I came to be here.

I tried to ferret in my mind for the last thing I could remember, but hard as I tried, I found I could not. There had been shouting, the clang of the ship's bell — which resulted in more shouting — and yet more of those terrifying noises. Explosions and *wheee* sounds and deafening crumps that sounded like the ship was being ripped and gored and beaten, the licks of flame, the sting of smoke thick and acrid on the air.

And then . . . what? What *had* happened? How had I come to be here? How *long* had I been here? I knew it was light — well, more a dove grey, from what little that I could see through the scuttle — but I realised I had no idea of time, of what day it was; no idea how long I might have slept. I felt sluggish, stiff and listless, as if I'd been asleep for a long time — a deep, dreamless sleep — having lain in an awkward position.

I lifted my nose to sniff the air again and immediately regretted it. For some reason it hurt to move my head. It hurt a *lot*, in fact; a tentative stretch of my neck immediately confirmed it, pain streaking through my hind legs with such heat and intensity that I knew I must be very badly hurt.

I stayed still, concentrating as hard as I could on not moving; despite the constant urge to shake the noise out of my ears. It helped that I was too scared to even try to see my injuries, so I lay rigid but inert, waiting for both my heart and my head to stop pounding, and for the pain to subside to something I could deal with.

And I would have dealt with it, had my slow slide back into painless oblivion not been arrested by the sound of a single, anguished moan, which seemed to be coming from somewhere close by. I thought I recognised the voice, too. Was it Lieutenant Weston's? Fear flooded in. Was he hurt? Had he been injured as well?

It all came back to me then, quickly, intensely and chillingly: the communists. The shells. The orders barked down the voice pipes. Bridge to wheelhouse. Full speed ahead! The *Amethyst* powering upriver, away from the first shore batteries, the captain not quite believing that what was happening *could* be happening; that we'd been anything other than simply caught in the crossfire between the communists and nationalists occupying the opposite shores.

And then the reality, quickly following the assumption that we'd passed the trouble: that, as we'd by now unfurled the Union Jacks the crew had made, there could be no question that they were firing on a British frigate. My padding down to the captain's cabin, half believing we might be clear of it, then the terrible, terrible sound from just above me — the cabin door slamming shut, and then almost immediately bursting open — the mushroom cloud of choking black smoke surging in. The realisation that they *had* meant to fire on us — that they were firing on us now; that they meant us grievous harm. The shock of it. The terror. The sense of disbelief and outrage. Of hearing the captain — no, that was wrong — it had been the first lieutenant, hadn't it? Of the first lieutenant, shouting . . . Return fire! Return fire! Bridge to wheelhouse! *Return fire!* Feet, thundering past me. Screams — so much screaming! Of the shouts and the cries — the desperate, keening cries — then the massive *whump!* close at hand, and the feeling that I was flying — of being lifted high, high, and higher, way up into the air, that same air then being violently snatched from my lungs . . .

The *explosion!* I juddered involuntarily, causing a second wave of agony to streak through my body, and the darkness sucked me down once again.

When I woke the second time, in stifling heat now, feeling thirsty and dizzy, it was to a second, even scarier revelation. It was one that I sensed, rather than saw, sniffing a sharp note of charring in the still air of the cabin and having it suddenly hit me what the source of the smell might be.

My whiskers! Where were my whiskers? Had they been burned off completely? I felt sick. I wanted to *be* sick, and even felt myself retching. For, despite my prone position, and my having no immediate need of them, the realisation of their absence felt like a violent wound itself. It terrified me anew. Would they ever grow back again? And what other grievous injuries might I have sustained?

I tried to lift my paw, very gingerly, the better to establish what I'd been left with, but again, the slightest movement — of *any* part of me, it seemed — caused me intense pain, and sent waves of nausea coursing through me. And as I could see almost nothing, I had no choice but to try to lie as still as I could again. To try to find refuge in further sleep.

But it was hard to sleep. The sound in my ears was like a burrowing animal worming away at me, and with so many questions swirling round my head, my brain was equally buzzing. What was going on? Where was everyone? What had become of Lieutenant Weston? What was happening to the *Amethyst*? Was she even moving?

My senses told me no, but they were muddled. Eventually I did sleep, though it was fitful enough and shallow enough to allow the noises around me to filter through. And the noises were, by now, at least a little less frightening, the screams and whumps of shells being replaced by very different sounds, a few of them even familiar and reassuring.

I thought I could hear the coxswain. Was that his low, phlegmy rasp? And Peggy? Was that Peggy barking? Oh, I hoped so. After a time, even more reassuringly, I could smell food being cooked, too, immediately conjuring the comforting image of one of my favourite spots in the galley, where I'd sit patiently while Slushy, the cook, trimmed what looked like whole sides of cows so they would fit into the oven, often treating me to a titbit of raw meat.

But such appearance of normality was soon unmasked as an imposter, and even in my weakened state, and with my mind bent so far out of shape by the constant noise in my head and the pain in my hindquarters, I recognised that despite the welcome clangs, thumps and whistles, things aboard the

Amethyst were very far from normal. Was the terrible thing that had happened to us still going on in some way?

I strained to make sense of some of the sounds that were reaching me; of men below and along the passageway making strange, mournful noises; of angry shouts; of muffled sobs; of a single, anguished scream from somewhere above. They must have eventually triggered something because more memories started rushing back towards me like a tidal wave surging over a beach. Of seeing things happening to my friends that seemed to defy belief and comprehension. Of men flailing and shouting, men falling and screaming. Of the acrid taste of smoke and cordite in the air. Of mangled lumps of metal strewn all over the *Amethyst*, as if flung there, like so much jagged jetsam.

But I mostly saw blood. Viscous, oily pools of it, steam rising from it, almost the colour of Cotton Tree blossom. I remembered lying on the quarterdeck, not understanding how I got there, and seeing *blood*, instead of water, flowing thickly across the deck and into the scuppers.

I closed my eyes again, hoping to make it all go away. But it wouldn't disappear. It seemed burned onto my brain.

"Well, now, look at this one. He really has been in the wars, hasn't he?"

I woke again with a start, feeling immediately anxious, because I was sure I could sense a stranger standing over me. It was the odour — strong and

104

musky, laced with some fuel-type tang I didn't recognise. It was alien enough to snap me into consciousness in a moment.

He spoke gently, however, and with a strange twang to his voice. It was a form of human speech that I hadn't heard before. Disorientated and confused, I tried to open my eyes so that I could see him, but found I couldn't. My eyelids seemed to be gummed shut. After a couple of painful attempts to part them, I gave up trying. Perhaps I should leave well alone.

"Something of a miracle he's still with us, I'd say, Doc, wouldn't you?"

My heart leaped. I knew that voice. It was Frank! It was *Frank*! I couldn't see him, but I was immeasurably glad to hear him.

I also registered that word "Doc". Was the man a doctor? "Sid Horton, one of the ratings, found him lying out on the deck this morning," Frank was explaining. "We suspect he was in the captain's cabin when it happened. Took a direct hit. He must have. You saw it, didn't you? When you came aboard? Beggars belief, it does." There was a pause. I tried to imagine their expressions. "Well, you could hardly miss it, could you?" Frank added at last. "Poor little blighter must have been blown feet in the air."

"So he's probably lost his hearing," the other man said, his odour mushrooming up around my face now, followed by the shock of feeling his fingers brushing against my fur. I tried to calm myself. He was a doctor. He was obviously taking a look at me.

"Oh, I don't think so, sir," Frank said. "I reckon he can hear us well enough, can't you, Simon?" To which I managed to respond with all I could manage — a feeble tail flick. It wasn't much — barely anything — but it seemed it was sufficient. "See, Doc!" said Frank. I could hear the pleasure in his voice.

"So he *can* hear," said the other man. "Well, well, well. And there's no blood in his ears, so that's good. Though that's a nasty burn on his left one, poor thing. But you've patched him up, I see." He touched me a second time. This time on my shoulder. "And that'll heal quick enough." There was another pause. "Anyway," he said finally. "As you say, something of a miracle."

"Did what we could," Frank said. "And if he's stayed with us this long, I reckon he'll be okay, don't you? Ship's cat, isn't he? Survivors. What's to say?" He cleared his throat. "Anyways, leave your things over there, and we'd best be getting you to the sick bay. The worst are gone, as you know, but we're far from doing well. Though there's a fair few in the after-mess as well." Yet another pause. He cleared his throat again. "We've run right out of room."

They left me then, and I could hear their steps echoing down the passageway. And they left me thinking. Yes, perhaps it *had* been a miracle.

Well, either that or I'd used up one of my nine lives.

CHAPTER
ELEVEN

Yangtse River, near Tan Ta Chen,
Friday 22 April, 1949

Following my visit from Frank and the man he'd called "Doc" the previous day (who turned out to be in the Air Force and was called Flight Lieutenant Fearnley), I had finally found the wherewithal to try to move. I had puzzled long and hard over why — and how — this doctor had come on board the *Amethyst*. How did he get to us? Or had the ship made it to Nanking without my realising? And where was our own doctor? Had he been injured as well? I didn't allow myself to consider the other possibility.

I hadn't moved much, not the first time, because it was still excruciatingly painful. Only sufficient to confirm what I already knew instinctively; that I'd been badly burned, and that my hips and back legs had been lacerated by pieces of shrapnel. Beyond that, I didn't know, and decided I didn't want to.

But I was alive, and could hear still — despite the persistent ringing — and my survival had been declared to be a miracle. I wondered if the rest of crew felt the same about it, and doubted it. As Frank had said, I was a ship's cat, and sailors were superstitious, believing not only in feline powers of survival that went far beyond the credible, but in our ability to keep the crew from harm, too.

I wished I'd never learned that, because the weight of it felt heavy on my shoulders, suffusing me with difficult, distressing feelings. What if I'd stayed up on the bridge? Would I still be here to ponder it? And what of the protection I was assumed to have conferred on the *Amethyst?* Where had that gone?

"You'll bring us luck, little feller!" I could hear dear George saying it. And that made me feel desperately sad.

I tried to console myself. George was safe somewhere else. Well, I hoped he was, anyway. I wondered where he was and what he might be doing now. And who knew? Had that luck — however scant, however tenuous — not been with us, perhaps even more would have perished. In any event, I felt humbled and all too aware of my *own* luck, and for those reasons knew I must bear my pain stoically. For in the time that had now passed since the explosion that had changed everything, I had learned of fates so much worse, so much more final, than mine.

Captain Skinner — brave Captain Skinner — was dead. I had already heard Petty Officer Griffiths discussing that with Lieutenant Weston in the adjacent wardroom; he'd died ashore, on the way to hospital. I'd also deduced — both from what they'd been saying and the way they'd been saying it — that Lieutenant Weston must be quite badly injured too.

Worse still, at least twelve of the crew were apparently dead also. Some had died instantly, some had been shot down in the water, one had died of his injuries on the way to the field hospital with Captain Skinner; others were still there now, badly wounded and shaken — some of them still at risk of dying too.

It was all such shocking news that I had not fully taken it in. Indeed, during the period when I was drifting in and out of consciousness in the cabin, I had hoped that the pictures that kept coming back to torture me were just the product of a fevered imagination. But they were not. They had happened.

I had managed to piece together some more of what had happened to the *Amethyst* simply by watching and listening. But it wasn't enough, and I felt useless and desperate for information, so much so that the previous night, in the eerily silent small hours, the *Amethyst* still motionless, I had finally dared test the limits of my strength and resolve again, and tried to leave the cabin to find out more.

I had made it further that time, but still not very far. In fact, dragging my stiffened limbs proved to be a little beyond that limit. By the time I had managed to make it out of Griffiths' cabin and into the passageway, such plans as I'd had, which were admittedly unformed to start with, became buried under fresh waves of pain.

Another thought had hit me then. I'd heard nothing of Petty Officer Griffiths since the previous day. Where might he be sleeping? *Was* he even sleeping? Was he safe? Something jerked inside me then — some primeval tug I had no control over. And I realised that whatever I had expected to achieve it was all cast aside. Instinct took over. A sudden, powerful, overwhelming instinct, as well: to hide away somewhere where nothing and no one could get to me, to find a place where I could retreat — where I could hide away, and curl up and retreat into myself; somewhere I could go and lick my wounds.

The ship had remained still. Still in the water, clearly anchored. I knew that she must have been still for some time, as well. It had been more than a day, in fact, since I'd last heard the throb of the engines, and, from the spot I'd found — behind a tangle of ropes in the corner of one of the forward gun decks — all I could hear above the whirr of bats and flying insects was the sound of the river lapping gently against the hull.

Here, gasping but finally on my side again, I was at least cooled a little by the corticene beneath me. Being able to see something other than a blank cabin wall was at least a distraction from the pain.

And what a distraction it turned out to be. Because the state of the *Amethyst* stunned me.

There was evidence of the shelling and machine-gunning everywhere — even the ensign flying at the stern hadn't escaped it. It flew limply, forlornly, stirred by only the smallest of breezes, half torn off and riddled with bullet holes.

But it was the *Amethyst*'s hull which horrified me the most. Always ghostly in the moonlight, she was now all sooty smudges — smudges that resolved themselves into evidence of major damage: scores of ragged scrapes and rents and gaping holes. One — the biggest I could

110

see from my vantage point — gaped high above me, just below the bridge, like a monstrous jaw. A blackened fissure, deep and shocking in the middle of the pristine whiteness, it was half-stuffed with what looked like piles of hammocks. It took a few moments for the realisation to sink. I realised with a gulp that I was looking at the captain's cabin.

I stayed laid up for the rest of that night and all the next morning, even when, at some time when the moon was high in the sky, wreathed in a yellowy mist, I felt the engines come to life again and the ship begin to move upriver. It wasn't for long, however, as very soon we were the target of yet more firing from the north bank — though as I lay there, it was without the least inclination to try to move, but simply to await whatever fate was now to befall me. I was done in. And now I was out here, there was nowhere to run to, even if I could. I'd stay put, I decided, and take my chances.

The gunshots, which had been sporadic, soon stopped altogether. I must have dozed then, despite everything (perhaps the vibration of the engines soothed me) and then slept more deeply, because when I woke up it was to a gradually lightening sky, and the boat was once again soundless and still.

The next thing I became aware of — again, some hours later — was the sound of an aircraft approaching. I had no idea at that point if that was a good thing or a bad thing, but I quickly had my answer. No sooner had it flown past us than I could hear firing from the shore again, and, after another burst of orders, shouts and clattering urgent footfalls, it was gone almost as quickly as it had arrived.

Fully awake again, I tried to take stock of things more clearly. To try to tease out the facts from the clues. We were motionless, but not docked, so we were obviously just anchored, presumably at some point further up the river. Though there was activity — hostile activity — from the north shore of the river, I could see or hear no other ships or sampans, so we seemed to be alone. And as it seemed that no other boat (or aircraft) was able to get close to us, I could only assume it was either because the *Amethyst* was physically unable to slip her mooring, or was being prevented from doing so in some other way.

I didn't have to think much to reach a single, obvious question. Were we stuck here because we were prisoners?

The day grew warm by increments, and very soon it was too hot to stay where I was. With the sun rising high in the sky, albeit partly masked by clouds, I knew the heat would shortly become intolerable. But I had another, much greater motivation to try to move. With so much going on that I was unable to see or hear properly, it was curiosity, as well as anxiety, which eventually dragged me from behind the rope coils — not least concerning the identity of a new arrival on the *Amethyst* an hour or so later. I'd heard a craft come alongside (probably a landing craft, I decided, due to the soft, purring engine) and, as I couldn't see it, I was anxious to know who or what it contained.

I made my way haltingly around the snakes of rope — stiff again from the long period of immobility — and tried to forget about my missing whiskers. But all my small trek achieved was to place me a little further along the gun deck, where I flopped down close to the guard rail, my back legs unable to carry me further, where I could at least pick up a little of what was happening.

It seemed as though an officer was coming aboard — I couldn't see him, but could tell from the tone of his voice, and the tone of voice of the man who was receiving him — another that I couldn't quite place. And as they headed inside — perhaps to the wireless room or the wardroom? — all I could pick up was that there was some sort of dispute going on. I heard the name Weston, and a while later, heard Lieutenant Weston himself, sounding strange and as if he was struggling to get his words out. "We've destroyed everything," he kept saying, over and over. "All the papers and the charts . . ." "I *know*, man. Calm yourself," the stranger reassured him. "I *am* calm," Weston kept saying. He was anything but.

Whoever had arrived hadn't been inside long, for in no time there were men back on the deck below me, their hushed exchanges floating up to me only in part. But then they moved, and I heard someone say very clearly, "There's no choice, man. If you don't get that shrapnel removed, you'll die!"

I lay back again then, trying to make sense of it. Was that the "doc" I had heard talking? Hard to say, but it was another voice I couldn't seem to place, and soon after, it was joined by the throb of the landing craft engine, which was presumably leaving us again. It was only when it had travelled some distance that I was able to catch sight of it. Though I couldn't be sure, I had enough of a glimpse to think it true — the landing craft was taking away Lieutenant Weston.

My first proper sighting of our new captain, a tall man called Lieutenant Commander Kerans, was when I limped onto one of the gun decks a few hours later, feeling compelled to find my friends again. And I found the ship's company (such as it was, for by now I knew many of my friends were probably missing, or injured and down in the sick berth) had been mustered to attend what was clearly a very sombre gathering. Judging from the light — a murky charcoal, which the sun struggled to penetrate — it was now late in the afternoon. It was the first time I'd seen most of them in three days.

It had been a long walk to rejoin my company, every step sending knives of pain shooting through my hindquarters, and I'd had to sink down and catch my breath often. My skin stung — it was now clear that I'd lost quite a lot of fur — and I was so parched that I'd been driven to cast around the deck and try to lick up any beads of moisture I could find. But the sound of voices drove me on, and after I had no idea how long, I was rewarded by the first glimpse of my friends.

I would make it to the end guardrail above the gun deck, I decided. I kept my eyes on it, as if it were some kind of prize, limping slowly along the hull, keeping close to the bulkhead, feeling my back legs at every step quivering and protesting beneath me, and eventually found myself looking down at a dizzying blur of white.

I blinked painfully, trying to reconcile what I was seeing with what had happened. To square what I'd heard and learned with what I gazed down upon now. The remaining crew — much reduced — were all decked out in their white uniforms. They looked crisp and impossibly shipshape in their finery, and, to a man, they stood rigid and unsmiling.

It was impossible not to contrast them with the post-attack *Amethyst*: wounded, broken, lying up — licking its own wounds. Yet here were so many of my dear friends, gathered upon her battered deck, almost like a flock of beautiful white birds. Yes, they were bent and broken too, but they were also standing tall, managing to find strength and dignity from somewhere.

All thoughts of my own pain were spirited away then, because it was only now that I realised what I was witnessing. For in his hands, our new captain held what I knew to be the ship's Bible.

Seeing that particular book lying open in his hands, I couldn't help but find my eyes drawn behind him, where a line of low, sheet-covered mounds stretched along the gun deck. My friends' bodies.

I couldn't take my eyes off them, not for a long time, struck by the precision with which they had been arranged, by their shape, by their stillness. Which were they? Who was missing from the assembly?

There were so many men missing — many more than this number, surely? — that, apart from those I knew about, it would be impossible to work out who had died these past three days. I would find out; that wretched information would all too soon be known to me. In the meantime, I must do the same as my friends below me. Pay my respects and wish them peace where they were going.

Heads were lowering now, and a new solemnity fell upon the gathering. As I watched and listened, the captain speaking in tones mostly too low for me to catch them, the first body was committed to the river by a burial party of four ashen-faced men. Familiar faces, one I recognised as one of the ordnance men, Leighton, whose job today was to lash one of his shells to each sailor, to weigh them down — a bitter irony indeed. By the time they were done, the sun had dipped below the horizon.

And the sailors laid to rest at the bottom of the Yangtse River had numbered seventeen.

CHAPTER
TWELVE

Though it seemed unimaginable for such a thing to happen, in the grim days that followed that terrible funeral service, I found myself grateful for the rats. For it was undoubtedly the rats — now my mortal enemy *and* my naval duty — that gave me the will to recover. I knew I *must* recover, at least enough to find the strength to hunt them down and, hopefully, kill enough of them to make it clear to the rest that they were not going to take over the *Amethyst*.

We were trapped on the Yangtse. That much had been easy to establish. Time and again, some effort was made to free the ship, and as sure as the sun rose every morning, hazy and ineffectual, we'd be fired on by the communists on the north bank. Even so, there was work to be done on deck — urgent work — so what was left of the crew (less than half the ship's company, I estimated) were labouring at all hours, courageously, right in the enemy's sights, doing what was needed to make the ship seaworthy again. They were stuffing sandbags into holes, piling flour sacks around the bridge and wheelhouse, clearing wreckage from the decks, pumping out water from the wardroom, and frantically jettisoning whatever could be jettisoned —

including oil — to try to get the ship back on an even keel.

What it seemed we weren't going to be able to do, though, was actually go anywhere. Which meant the *Amethyst* had, to all intents, been captured by Mao Tse-tung's men, even if they hadn't boarded us, and would remain where she was till they decreed it otherwise.

Much as I craved their company, I stayed hidden from my friends for several days. Unable to walk properly, and fearful of being touched — even in kindness — I knew the best thing would be to keep myself out of sight and out of the way until I was strong enough to resume my own duties. So in the days and nights that followed I tried to keep to the shadows and secret places — an observer until I was healed enough to be anything else.

Everyone still on board seemed in shock, just like I was. Bar Peggy, who, being a dog, skipped around with her usual abandon, there wasn't a crew member on board who didn't look traumatised and exhausted.

I'd not seen Jack at the funeral, and I feared for him. I could only hope that he was in the wireless room, as reason told me he would be, busy tap-tapping away, sending his signals to the admiral, relaying whatever messages our new captain required.

I feared for *all* my friends, be they injured or able-bodied, on board or otherwise. I felt their pain. Which, having been born a solitary creature, was a strange new sensation for me. And it struck me how particularly wretched it must be for the fifteen young boy sailors who'd joined us just a month back, who, when out on deck, thin as reeds and as pale as the moonlight, looked so wide-eyed and jittery and terrified.

It was perhaps three or four days after the attack when it hit me why. It was when I watched the usual detail — the mop and bucket men who usually took such pleasure in their good-natured teasing — come out onto the quarterdeck and start scrubbing away at the corticene, and in such a fury that at first I thought they must be on a charge over some transgression. Then I noticed something not previously evident from where I was sitting: that what they were scrubbing away at, with their buckets of steaming, frothing water, was not the usual sooty deck grime, but blood.

If I hadn't seen that red water run in streams into the scuppers, I imagine I would very soon have worked it out anyway. What I'd misread as fury was actually pain; pain not only evident from the grisly task they were detailed to perform, but from the tears streaming down the young ratings' cheeks.

There was nothing in the world short of physical impossibility that would prevent me from doing what I could to help, though I soon realised that I would have my work cut out.

First of all, I was missing half my whiskers. I was missing half my eyebrows, and a great deal of fur from my hindquarters, too, but it was the damage to my whiskers, which had all but been burned off in the explosion, that distressed me the most.

I had known this from the outset, of course, because it would be impossible not to, but now their loss anguished me anew. It was one thing to move around all the familiar lighted places, but now I was keen to hunt again, I was doubly bereft to be without them as, when night fell — and particularly in the dark places below — I found it so much harder to see.

But see I must — and as a matter of urgency, too — because the rats, who must have rubbed their nasty little claws together in spiteful glee, had become bolder than at any time since I'd joined the crew of the *Amethyst*. As I lay up, cleaning my wounds, trying to will myself stronger, I could hear them moving about the ship, creeping and scuttling and defecating along their rat runs — an advancing horde (much like Mao Tse-tung's communists, I thought grimly) with just one thing on their minds. The spoiling and purloining of our now doubly precious stores.

I made my first rat-catching foray in the small hours of the night. The ship, always sleepy at this hour, was preternaturally still, with just the slap of river water sploshing weakly against the hull and the ever-present drone of the night insects.

I took a route I knew well: past the wardroom, down to the galley, through the tight space between the ovens, then down to the very back of the stores, where everything ahead of me was solid black. And oh, how I felt crippled without my whiskers to help guide me, constantly having to stop and nudge my nose up to make up for the unsettling loss of vision.

120

I hobbled. Doubly lame. Like a blind animal in a blind alley. And because no one had ever told me, I had no idea when, or even if, new whiskers might start growing. I could only trust in logic, albeit without a great deal of confidence, and hope that they would grow again, and soon.

I padded on doggedly, and at last I caught a strong rodent scent — strong enough to have me quivering with anticipation, and pausing to take both stock and soundings. And almost immediately after that came the all-too-familiar scufflings and scratchings of a rat dining on food that didn't belong to it.

I slunk round a pipe then, cold against me, and at last spied my prize. And when I fixed it in my vision (albeit hazily, without the reassuring confirmation from my whiskers) I sank down again slowly, trying to focus; trying to ignore the scream of protest in my hips. Whatever I currently lacked, I reminded myself firmly, one advantage I did have was my silence — my ability to stalk prey without creating so much as a whisper of unsettled air.

But there was no point in lingering. I would only stiffen up. I tensed myself and sprang.

And, to my horror, I missed. My claws found nothing more substantial than a scrape of scaly tail, and even that, as if to taunt me, caught my ear like a whiplash, as the filthy animal made good its escape.

There was no getting away from it. I felt desperately sorry for myself. My body ached, my ear hurt — the rat must have caught the spot that had been burned already — and it took some minutes before I was able to properly catch my breath.

Worse still, though, were the thoughts swirling in my head, which, like the rat, seemed to mock me for my arrogance. What had possessed me? I was in no fit state to hunt — even a cockroach could now evade me — and I had no idea when or if I would be. I had gone, at a stroke, from being a valued crew member to a burden, a useless liability to my friends. And as I made my way forward, with no clear idea where next to lie, I felt the welling of shame stinging my eyes and my gait becoming sluggish — as if grinding to a halt, much like the *Amethyst* herself, a prisoner of my own feeble state.

Thank God for my ears, though. At least they hadn't failed me, and for the noise that, though distant, was caught by them now. I turned my head a little. Listened hard. It was regular. Tinny. And I realised — daring to hope now, my failure all but forgotten — that it was coming from the wireless room. Was it Jack?

I limped off to find out, climbing awkwardly over the barriers beneath the doorways, which, it seemed to me, had almost doubled in size. But as I neared the noise, the deficiencies of my hind legs mattered less to me, with my only goal — my only *need* — being to know if Jack was alright.

I halted, however, just a few yards from the wireless room, confused by what looked like sacks of flour arranged around it. Had it suffered terrible damage? Was it flooded? No longer in use? But as I sat there, uncertain, I realised I could hear voices — ones that

122

seemed to be coming from inside the room, talking urgently.

"So, this to C in C." Was that Captain Kerans speaking? He reeled off a message about deadlocks and meetings. From his tone it was obvious he wasn't very happy. "Quick as you can, Flags," he finished. I imagined Jack (let it be Jack!) scribbling furiously with his pencil, ready to turn the message the captain had given him into Morse code.

Then came Lieutenant Hett's voice, as ever, deep, clear and strong. "I'll have Lieutenant Fearnley give you something," he said. "Some more Benzedrine will help, lad. And what about some food, eh? When did you last eat?"

"I'm not hungry, sir. I'm fine. Just the Benzedrine'll be fine, sir."

It was Jack's voice! It *was* Jack! I was so excited I almost forgot myself, emerging from the shadows and only narrowly avoiding cannoning into the captain and lieutenant as they swept out of the room and hurried off back to the bridge.

The wireless room was warm and looked untouched by the shelling; still humming and cosy and exactly as it always was, a constant in a world that had been so changed.

Jack was alone, with his back to me, busy working on the message at his little fold-down desk. As I entered he straightened, pulled his Morse code machine towards him, and began tapping out the message in that curious staccato rhythm that "another Jack", he'd explained to me, "will hear through his earphones, translate, and write down — and that's it — job done. Bob's your uncle!"

I sat back on my haunches, carefully, and waited for him to finish, only going to him once he peeled his headphones from his ears, and stuck the pencil back in place over the right one.

Then I mewled. He looked down. Then he blinked. Then his mouth gaped. "Blackie!" he exclaimed, pushing his chair back and patting his knees. "Love a duck! Where've you *been*? We thought we'd lost you!"

I couldn't jump. Didn't try. Didn't dare. He quickly realised. He bent down, and as he did so, he let out a heavy groaning sigh.

"Aww, look at the state of you," he said, picking me up very gingerly by cupping his hands around my front legs. "You okay, boy? When d'you last eat? You're skin and bone. Look at you . . ." He gently turned me this way and that, so he could get a better look at me, and I forced myself to cope with the pain even this small movement gave me — it didn't matter. I was just so grateful for the comfort of his touch.

I studied Jack too. He looked exhausted. His skin was the colour of paper. I wondered when he had last eaten, as well. "Those ruddy bast — 'scuse my French, Blackie, but look what those *bastards* have done to you! Here, sit yourself down. That's the way. That's the way. *Lord*, it's good to see you. Been getting awful lonely sitting in here, hour after hour, all on my lonesome." He grimaced. "'S only me now, my friend. Ruddy commies got the others. Just me now. Been up round the clock for ruddy days now." He laid a hand on my head, taking care to mind my ear. "Oh, it's so good to see you. We all thought you'd bought it. Taken yourself off and died somewhere, we thought — and here you are! You're a sight for sore eyes, you know that?" Then he suddenly leaned forward. "Eh oh. Here we go. Hang on, Blackie. Let's get this down, eh?" Then he pulled the chair up to the desk again, plonked his earphones on his head, and began transcribing the reply to the message the captain had sent, while I sat in his lap, feeling warm and safe and humbled.

CHAPTER
THIRTEEN

Sound asleep on Jack's lap that night, I dreamed of my mother. She was on the *Amethyst*, alongside me, my protector and friend, and when a machine gun was fired at us from a battery on a shore — the bank flocked with the enemy, all shouting and raging — she sprang up and took the bullets for me, falling lifeless at my feet. A bloom of blood then grew beneath her, till the tug of gravity took it, and it rushed in a stream into the scuppers.

I woke with a start, to the sound of voices again, but this time they were low and conspiratorial. Trying to shake the horrible images from my head, I opened my eyes, to see Lieutenant Hett and the man Frank had called Doc standing over us, the latter with a plate of sandwiches in his hand.

Lieutenant Hett smiled and raised a finger. "Shh . . ." he mouthed more than said to me. It was then that I realised that Jack was fast asleep. His head was resting on his arm, which was flat across his desk now, and had formed a cosy human tent for me to doze under. I realised the rhythm of his breathing; it was the same one that must have rocked me to sleep.

"Good to see you again, little fella," the one called Doc whispered. Again I wondered. Was he here because Doctor Alderton was injured? And where was Thomas, the sick bay attendant? I'd not seen him either.

The doc turned to Hett and nodded, and they both moved further away. "I don't mind staying in here for a bit," he said, keeping his mouth close to the lieutenant's ear. "Let him sleep. He's done in. He can take more Benzedrine later. I can wake him up soon enough if anything new comes in."

Hett nodded. "Good man. I'll send a cuppa down for you when it's brewed then." Then he turned back to me. "How about you, Simon? Peckish, old son?" He came back and crouched down so he was on my level. "My, boy, you look like you've been existing on thin air!"

I doubted anything would have woken Jack, but I took the utmost care in any case, slithering down from his lap as carefully and smoothly as I could. Then, with a wobble of my hindquarters, which I quickly corrected, padded across to say hello to my lieutenant friend. "Some sardines, eh?" he whispered. He looked amused. Pleased to see me. "Least the rats can't get their filthy teeth into the tins, eh? Well —" he grimaced. "Not yet, anyway. Way they're going, I wouldn't put it past them."

I pressed myself around his shin, purring, then wound a slow double figure of eight around the pair of them, to let them know just how pleased I was to see them as well. Then I padded off, over the threshold and back to the dark, infested places. I would love some sardines. My mouth watered at the prospect. It was the first time I'd thought of anything but pain and thirst in all these days.

I would *love* some sardines. A plate of herrings out, too. Or herrings *in*, even. The kind in the horrible sauce Jack favoured. *That* was how hungry I suddenly found myself. I held onto the thought.

Then I tilted my nose, sniffed the air, caught a scent and began to follow. No doubt about it. I would love some sardines. I really would. But not just yet. First I was going to *earn* them.

Hunger and fury are a potent combination. That and the power of friendship. I was *not* going to let my friends down.

I killed two rats that night. Though at some cost to myself, admittedly. The second, a big ugly brute of a male, made a swipe that tore open the wound in my ear — *again* — and made it bleed so much it dripped all down my face.

But such was my delight — and relief — at having dispatched the hated animals that it could have bled all the next day (and might well have, had Petty Officer Frank not managed to staunch it) and I wouldn't have cared. As it was, I was exhausted, but it was a good kind of weariness. The weariness of a job done to the best of my abilities and more than that, proof that where there is a will, there is, almost always, a way. I had Jack's devotion to his own duty to thank for that.

I delivered my trophies, one by one, as naval protocol dictated — the first, at dawn, to the captain's bunk —

he being apparently busy inspecting the boilers. I'd yet to properly meet him and was keen to assure him that I was anxious to do my bit. I hoped he'd be pleased, and spent time arranging the rat's body just so, before padding back to resume my duties below. My second catch, just an hour later, I decided would be for Jack, to cheer him up while he toiled at his post in the wireless room. He was by now wide awake again, looking all the better for his sleep, and munching on one of his "herrings in" sandwiches.

He looked almost bug-eyed, in fact — like one of the black beetles that used to cling to the banyan fronds at dusk — when I padded in with my kill, saying, "That is the *best* thing I've seen in days!" He immediately leaned across to send a message up the voice pipe, shouting, "Wireless room to engine room! Guess what. Blackie's killed a flippin' monster!", upon which a message came back, almost immediately. "Er, correction, Flags — he's actually killed two!"

It was the captain's voice. He'd obviously found it. I couldn't have felt more proud. Or, indeed, more hungry. When I was presented with the promised plate of sardines shortly afterwards, I ate them so fast that Jack even whistled his admiration up the voice pipe. "Gone almost before you could say Jack Robinson, sir!" he told the captain.

Whoever Jack Robinson was. I felt proud of that, as well.

But, in reality, there was little room for pride on board the *Amethyst*. Not as things stood. As I patrolled the ship over the next couple of days, full of emotion, full of respect, it was clear that, for all the camaraderie, the crew were not just physically exhausted, they were emotionally exhausted too, grieving for and mourning their dead friends. Most of all, again and again, it confirmed my first impression: that just as the memory of my mother's brutal death would always haunt me, so the faces of the crew — particularly the youngest, most inexperienced seamen — wore the pain and revulsion of the things they had witnessed, their brows etched not just with lines made of oil and grease and soot, but by the business of remembering, and the distress it must cause them. I felt for them. Grieved with them. Wished I could better help them, but knew I could not.

It was Peggy — dear, silly, muddle-headed Peggy — who first showed me that I was quite wrong about that. Something that should have been as clear as the nose on my face: that I could do so much more than just deal with the rat colony for my friends. I could help them in other ways, too.

It was a few days later, and I was patrolling the rat runs, as focused as ever, as, with no sign of us being allowed to continue on our journey to Nanking, it seemed we could be stuck for some time.

And it hadn't just been the two kills that had fired me with such ambition. It was the fact that the rats were becoming their own worst enemies. So emboldened had they become since the ship had been marooned that they were often to be seen scuttling along their rat runs in broad daylight, as if — or so they thought — they had nothing to fear!

130

One of their runs ran through the sick bay, and was becoming increasingly well travelled, doubtless providing some new and devious rodent short cut to the already diminishing stores. There was sufficient food as yet — plenty of preserved food, and a reasonable stock of dry goods — but without fresh food of any kind, bar what could be obtained from the nationalists, the dry goods were an increasingly precious commodity. They had become currency, and could be traded for potatoes, greens, and eggs.

But it was that same store of dry goods — flour and cereals and rice, and so on — that the rats were most intent on stealing from under us, and what they didn't steal, they spoiled, rendering it useless. Because there was also the health risk, which was not something I knew much about, admittedly, but the new doctor was clear on the dire threat they posed. Rats spread disease and the rat population was growing. I had never been more needed and my injuries seemed as nothing in the face of it.

Peggy was in the sick bay, on a bunk, sitting squarely on someone's chest. Which was an arresting enough sight in itself. She barked when she saw me (being entirely without any sort of hunting instinct, she could scatter prey in an instant) and the sailor turned around and grinned at me.

I didn't know him well — he was one of the young lads that had only joined the *Amethyst* recently — but the smoothness of his skin under the sweat and grime was telling.

There was a bucket beside the bunk and as he had no visible injuries, I suspected he must have gone down with an infection of some kind — one of those "health risks" our new doctor kept muttering about to the captain, while exhorting the men to wash and clean and scrub.

"It's the hero of the hour!" he said. His face was greyish. Gaunt and angular. "Come here, little man," he coaxed, "come and have a cuddle with me and Peg, eh?" He hung an arm down at the side of the bunk to coax me, while Peggy licked his face.

I duly trotted across, noticing as I did so how strange the sick bay smelled now. It was a new smell; sharply acid, and oddly sweet, too, and as I inhaled it I remembered something I'd previously forgotten — the frantic panic, the screaming, the desperate cries of "Get him in! Get him in!". It was only a wisp of memory, a snatch of something I'd prefer to bury, but the scene, even though I couldn't quite see it, became clearer. This same sick bay, not so long ago, would have been full of horribly wounded sailors, with our doctor — I'd now learned he'd been slain, along with his assistant, Thomas — dashing around desperately, trying to do what he could for his men, slipping and sliding on the pools of spilled blood . . .

Wash, clean and scrub, I thought. *Wash, clean and scrub*. Once the surviving wounded were taken away and driven to hospital, the sick bay — scene of so much carnage — must have been one of the first priorities. No such care and attention for my mother, whose body had no choice but to stay where it had been flung. I'd had to find a new route across the island from that day.

Today, the sick bay was clean, neat and bright, and almost empty. Bar this one young sailor, and a rating in bed in the far corner, who was snoring, the only other patients were ghosts.

I nudged my head into the sailor's hand, feeling sadness pressing down on me, and though I braced for the pain as he brushed my still scabby ear, none came. His touch was as light as a cloud.

I managed to jump up onto the bunk, which was happily low, feeling extremely thankful for the growing strength in my back legs. And as I padded up the blanket, Peggy woofed, just a low, gentle snicker. And then stuck her great black wet nose into my face.

"Look at you two," the young sailor said, in his high but rasping voice. "Who'd have thought a cat and dog would ever get on like you do?" Who indeed? I thought, as Peggy hopped down and trotted off to make room for me. "Here you go, then," said the sailor. "Have the warm spot, why don't you?"

I settled down in the space Peggy had just vacated, and kneaded my claws into the rough grey of the blanket. "Aren't I the lucky one?" the sailor said, a smile stretching his tired features. "I could get used to this, I could. I *well* could . . ." And within what seemed like mere moments, his eyes had fluttered closed, and his breathing had become slow and regular. Every once in a while, the corners of his mouth would twitch a little. Happy dreams? I hoped so. To chase away the nightmares.

CHAPTER
FOURTEEN

It was several days before I was to gain any real understanding of why we were still trapped halfway up the Yangtse. After the usual Sunday morning church service, the crew were told to gather on the lower mess deck, and once Captain Kerans had all the men assembled together, he explained that we were in the middle of what he called a "diplomatic deadlock". The local garrison commander, who had authority over the shore batteries that had fired on us, was not prepared to let us go.

Peggy and I sat together on one of the gun decks, the watery sun like a blanket on our backs, watching the antics of a small group of plump brown and white birds, who were bobbing on the water a few yards from the *Amethyst*, poking through the surface with their pencil-like beaks.

I couldn't help but contrast the scene with the starkness of the captain's words. "If we attempt to move, we will be fired upon," he explained grimly. "Until such time as we are prepared to admit that the *Amethyst* fired first."

There was a swell of angry protest at this outrage. He raised a hand to silence it. "Which I have, of course, *emphatically* denied. And shall continue to do so, as we are not in the business of colluding with such lies. Quite apart from anything else, it would be a gross betrayal of the men who have died here. But I'm afraid that leaves us in something of a bind, and I'm going to need you all to be strong. As of now, we are in reasonably good shape. Talks continue — agonisingly slowly, but they continue — and at the highest level, so I am at least hopeful that it won't be too long before the communist leaders take heed of the truth — that there is a somewhat trigger-happy garrison commander at the root of this mess — and that we'll be allowed to continue our journey to Nanking.

"But, in truth, I cannot say how long things will take. So though we must hope for the best, we must also prepare for the worst. Keep occupied, do everything we can to make the *Amethyst* seaworthy, and be understanding about the difficulties and privations that may lie ahead. We are at least lucky that we have assistance from the nationalists and can get our hands on some fresh food, though with the communists taking control of both banks of the river now, in places, I don't know how long that might continue. We must also preserve our oil, for obvious reasons, so frugality is going to be key. To that end, I'm going to review our use of it on a day-by-day basis. It may well be that at some point soon we'll have to shut down the boilers at night. Which won't be comfortable, especially with the temperatures rising as they are, but I know I can rely on you all to be stoical."

The captain knew he could also rely on me doing my part. Since the first rat I'd given him, I'd caught another two, and though our paths hadn't crossed much he'd spotted me the previous morning and to my delight had said, "Well, now — so this is our master rat-catcher! Very glad to make your acquaintance at last, young Simon. Keep up the good work!" Then he'd smiled and strode off, hands clasped loosely behind his back, leaving me puffed up with pride.

He looked around at the crew now and, following his gaze, so did I. So many of the remaining crew were so young themselves, and it shook me. Not to mention Lieutenant Strain, the fleet's electrical officer, who now looked every inch the weather-beaten sea dog, despite having only joined the *Amethyst* at Shanghai the night we'd sailed — a taxi ride to Nanking was all he'd been after. As it stood, he'd been lucky to survive.

"As I say, men," Captain Kerans finished, "this is a difficult situation — and one not of *any* of our making. And all we can do is accept our place in it with fortitude, and trust that everything that can be done *is* being done to expedite our safe passage. In the meantime, I know Lieutenant Commander Skinner would have been extremely proud of you. As am I. You are a credit to His Majesty's Navy."

Captain Kerans had the men fall out then, and despite the morale-boosting words, it was clear that the reality of our capture was beginning to sink in, and the mood quickly dipped again. I could see it in the slump of shoulders as the crew dispersed, in the low mutterings of discontent that floated up to me and Peggy.

I could mostly sense the growing anger, which was wholly justified, that the *Amethyst* was being pinpointed as the aggressor. That to admit to an outright lie would be a condition of us being freed, just to save the face — and perhaps the bacon — of a communist soldier who'd done wrong. And that anger was good, I thought. Fortifying and good. It would give the men a much needed reason to stay strong.

But it seemed Captain Kerans had been right when he'd used the words "agonisingly slowly". A week passed and then another, and a new routine became established; one of hard physical work to keep the *Amethyst* in peak condition, which meant maintenance and cleaning and drills for the men, and round-the-clock rat-hunting for me. And while we got on with the business of managing our silent, stranded ship, the officers would be back and forth across the Yangtse in a communist sampan, back and forth, back and forth, all done up in their whites — to meetings with the communists, which always promised much but in every case failed to deliver.

The weather was a constant irritant too. The temperature rose and kept rising, but more often than not, there was no pleasure to be had from it. "There's just too damned *much* weather!" Frank was moved to comment one day, as we were treated to lashings of rain and winds strong enough to blow a man right off his feet (let alone a cat) alongside the inevitable soaring temperatures, dense, swirling mists, and humidity so high it made everything wringing wet anyway. "Can't we just have one ruddy type at a time?"

And then, perhaps inevitably, came the news from the captain that in order to preserve the precious stock of oil we still had, the boilers would be shut down at night. This left nothing but the emergency lighting to rely on, and also meant there was no ventilation.

The news was greeted with grim acceptance, as the anger still held sway. They would not beat us. However hard they conspired to make life difficult for us, the truth was the truth, and every man was going to stick by it. To collude with their lies would be to betray our dead friends, so they could do what they liked.

Naturally, the rats were thrilled to bits.

CHAPTER
FIFTEEN

By mid-June, the temperature on board was becoming unbearably hot. By day it was in the hundreds and by night, not much cooler, and with the oil situation critical and no guarantee of getting more, the boilers remained shut down and silent every night, making the *Amethyst* as quiet as the grave.

It was strange and unsettling. A ship was a living, breathing thing. Whether at sea or in port, it was never meant to be completely silent. I knew this from my days as a kitten in Hong Kong. I would be mesmerised at night, often, by the big ships in the harbour — always lights showing, bells and whistles, the low chug and throb of all the engines and boilers, sailors running around everywhere, blurs of navy, flashes of white — seeming to crawl over the infrastructure like ants. This silence was different. It was complete and unbroken, and it was only now I felt it that I realised how peculiar it was.

I suspected the silence was the last thing on my friends' minds. Just the heat, and the humidity, and the inability to sleep; so much so that little by little, the sleeping arrangements changed. Forced to swelter and sweat through the long sticky nights, many would often give up their hammocks and sleep on camp beds out on deck.

Sleeping on deck became popular for other reasons too; the fact that the ship — now such a hothouse, due to the necessary lack of ventilation — was becoming infested with insects. Mosquitoes hid everywhere — they were extremely good at hiding — and stalked their prey with commando-like precision. I was lucky, as was Peggy — they had no interest in us — but the men were plagued constantly, many of them covered in angry — looking bites, and driven to distraction by the constant itching of them.

There was also a big increase in the cockroach population. Where toying with a cockroach had once been a happy diversion for me, there were now so many running around that I scarcely registered them, even when they twitched my finally sprouting whiskers. Where the rats had their runs, so the cockroaches did too, though where the rat runs followed routes behind pipes and under furniture, the cockroaches — nimble, quick, and entirely without limits — would scuttle along bedsteads and hammock ropes and pillowslips, and if a human got in the way they'd just scuttle straight over them, their antennae waving gaily as they passed.

It was an education in the curious sensibilities of humans; I knew cockroaches were high on the doc's list of "health crises in the making" because, like rats, they spread diseases. But it turned out the sailors didn't care about that. No. In the main, they were just very, very frightened of them. There was no logic in this. Not that

I could see, anyway. Yet the sight of a cockroach would have the biggest, burliest seaman shuddering — especially the younger ones — and I wasn't sure they knew why themselves. But what was very clear was that they found it impossible to ignore them. If they weren't jumping up and down on them — though *never* in bare feet — they'd be springing up, going "aagh!" and "yuck!" and "ruddy bleeders! Yarggg!", shaking themselves down as if they were crawling with scores of them, rather than just one, and doing strange little dances on the spot.

There was an entirely different attitude towards the moths. Strangely, given that moths were far superior when it came to flying (and often sat for minutes at a time on the men's faces, when they dozed off, if only they knew) they attracted nothing like the same frantic response. A moth was looked upon benignly, brushed away relatively calmly — though as the weeks passed and the heat grew their numbers began increasing, the cry of "Cover that ruddy light off — we'll be swamped with the bloody things!" became a common one.

But it was the rats — always the rats — who were posing the worst infestation, and by mid-June — six whole weeks since we'd been taken hostage by the communists — there was little choice but to stop using the aft part of the ship entirely, and let the rodents have the run of the place.

As a consequence, the men were even more crammed together in the heat and, when not working or on watch (Captain Kerans was becoming infamous for his "obsession" with keeping everyone occupied) attempted to amuse themselves not only by reading, or playing cards (or, touchingly, writing long letters that couldn't be posted) but by thinking up ways the evil scourge could be exterminated. Whenever the opportunity arose, boots were lobbed at any rat who was bold enough to run around in daylight.

These days, such boldness was common to most of them, and all I could do was my best. But it was fast becoming an unequal battle. I made kills every day now — rats were there for the taking — but for every one I finished off there seemed to be a dozen more.

"Breeding like rabbits!" Sid observed one evening, after the meal was cleared away. "We'll soon be overrun with the wretched things!

Sid, the youngest rating, had recently become a particular friend. To add to the woes already heaped on us by the communists, he'd suffered an injury a few weeks back when trying to adjust a steel cable. When he'd been taken ashore by the doctor, it was discovered he'd broken his arm, so he'd been in need of a little extra help and comfort.

I was sharing his hammock in the mess now, curled on top of his feet to keep his toes warm and, despite the chatter of the men, it was impossible not to hear the rats' constant scurryings and scrapings beneath and around us.

"Wish they *were* rabbits," remarked the other boy sailor, Martin. "Least then we could put them in a pie and eat the blighters!"

Martin, too, had had a tougher time than most. He and Bannister, one of the stoker mechanics, had been among those put to shore. They'd spent time in captivity — the plan being to use them to help coerce the captain. But they hadn't co-operated, and had not long been returned.

"Oh, for pity's sake!" said Sid. "Now you're making me feel sick!"

Sid was particularly queasy about the rats, having woken up one morning to find one half dead and squealing, dangling a scant three inches above his head, after a kind soul had rigged up a snare with some fuse wire. "Well, how was I to know you planned to sleep there?" the sailor had huffed.

As it was, my kills were mostly lobbed over the guardrail into the Yangtse. It became the ritual to wish them a safe journey to the north shore, where the "bloody commies" could roast them for dinner. I worked hard to keep the supply up, knowing my contribution was vital, as no other method of killing them seemed to work. Which was not to say the men didn't try — in a fit of furious determination upwards of fifty traps were laid in a single afternoon. The next day, not a single one was sprung.

It was perhaps inevitable, then, that the feeling became prevalent that the rats were more organised than we knew. They certainly seemed so — and so confident! They were increasingly bolder and braver. Poor Sid, who'd been dozing in the sick bay one afternoon, just after his accident, was roused from his slumbers by one calmly nibbling at his toes.

There was also talk of several sightings of a rat to beat the lot of them — a giant of an animal who they'd nicknamed Mao Tse-tung, on account of him seeming to be the ringleader. "Big as you, he is Blackie," Jack had helpfully told me. "I reckon you'd have a job on your hands, taking him on."

"Nah, he's a sight bigger," Sid had even more helpfully corrected him. "Job on his hands? I reckon that rat could see him off if he wasn't careful. You'd best keep away from him, Blackie."

"He's the one, though," Martin agreed. "He's the King Rat, no doubt about it. He's the one that needs dispatching to the afterlife, the filthy bugger. Before he sires any more of the blasted things."

I'd never thought about rats having an afterlife before. Did they too have their souls in the stars? I wasn't sure I liked it, but I had to concede that the idea made some sense to me, even it didn't inspire any finer feelings for the filthy vermin. I was a member of His Majesty's Navy and I had no time for that. Not for animals that caused so much misery for my friends.

I did think quite a lot about this legendary Mao Tse-tung, though. That perhaps Jack and Sid were right. Perhaps he would be too much for me. I'd already dealt with a couple of sizeable males, and, even with my strength returning and my whiskers coming along nicely, I was not fully fit yet, and it had been no small matter to catch them and finish them off. It seemed the bolder they got, the more well fed they got — while the men faced the meat running out in a matter of days now, the rats, gorging on grain and rice, were growing ever plumper. The plumper they were, the heavier and bulkier they were, and though I was healing

144

well — barely limping now, as Lieutenant Hett had noticed recently — I weighed no more than I ever did, nor, I thought, would I.

But for all my ever-present anxiety about facing down the fabled "King Rat", when the day of reckoning came, I had no time to even *think*, much less be frightened. It was all just so sudden, so unexpected, so unlike any rat encounter before it.

I had simply turned a corner onto the quarterdeck one morning, and there he was — it *had* to be him — looking as bold as you like. He was waddling across the deck in my direction, staying close to the bulkhead, but seemingly oblivious of all the sailors milling about, getting on with their duties. At first I could only gawp. He had such a proprietorial air about him (or so *he* thought; a rat could never aspire to such a thing) it really was as if he was entirely without a care. King Rat. Afraid of nothing and no one.

I'd sunk down to my belly before I'd even consciously thought about it, my instinct kicking in before my eyes had even registered what I'd seen.

He stopped too, and stared at me, his dead eyes like fish eyes. The same dull, unblinking gaze of a sandfish on a slab. His whiskers, in contrast, were quivering and questing, causing the air between us, which carried the scent of him, to tickle my own. He was a brute and his stench made me nauseous.

Jack had been right, though. Sid even righter. He was a *very* big rat. Even face on he looked huge so, though I couldn't properly see the length and spread of him, there was no question that he was almost as big as I

145

was. Not *as* big, which I registered gratefully, even as I stared. But heavier. So much heavier. A fat rat indeed. An unwelcome glimpse of the tip of his tail soon confirmed it. It was a good foot beyond the end of his body.

I settled and I watched and I waited, as per usual, vaguely conscious of movement at the edges of my vision. The men on deck had now noticed him too.

"Go on, Blackie," I heard someone say to me — in no more than a whisper, though my fear that it might give the rat cause to turn and flee was soon forgotten. Quite the opposite. He was actually edging *towards* me.

I stayed where I was, mindful of the things my mother had always warned me. With an animal this size, it would be foolhardy to ignore them. He rose up as he kept moving forward — though not in a straight line but using a strange angled walk. Then I realised. He was circling me. Trying to come around the side of me. The better to spring? Then I must get the advantage and spring first. I side-stepped, and now I *could* see the bulk of his body, but with my adrenaline pumping and my hackles fast rising, there was no question of *not* taking him on, giant though he was. I had my friends to think about. I could not, *would* not, walk away.

He slipped past me again, and I was treated to a flash of his rodent teeth. Huge pegs, they were. Perhaps the biggest I'd yet seen. Deep yellow, curving up to the roof of his mouth. I would have to spring and get my jaw locked high up on his neck. I spun around, sprang and pounced — no room for waiting, too dangerous — and in one move had my own teeth buried deep into the fur of his upper back.

He whirled then, unbalancing me, sending me over onto my flank, heavily, so I curled my paws round him to stop him gouging at my eyes. And he squealed and squealed and squealed — high, high, and higher, scrabbling and pulling me round with him, using all his strength, which was considerable, to free his front legs. My jaws were on fire from the extent I'd had to open them, my breath coming in rasps as I tried to keep them locked. I couldn't stand up and, even if I could, I hardly dared to — I knew it would only take the tiniest amount of slackening and he'd be out, he'd be free, he'd be turning on me . . .

I willed myself to bite down even harder — to try to finish him off now, to try to get a better, stronger, purchase . . . But the action only made him squeal and scrabble at me all the louder and harder. There was nothing for it — I had to clamp him between my paws and change my bite . . . One, two, three . . . Do it *now*. *Do it now!* Break and clamp. Break and grab again . . . Fast as you can. Strong as you can. *Do it!*

So I did it, and he jerked as if he were a lizard struck by lightning. And with my jaw screaming in pain now, I came *so* close to losing him, so stunned and unbalanced was I by the strength he had left. But then I felt it — the soft crack of his neck, then the stillness. Even then, for the longest time, I stayed as I was, panting, still as night, still as death, not once daring to loosen my grip. It must have been a full minute before

I judged it safe to release him, and let his body drop heavily between my paws.

"He's done it! He's done it! He's only gone and done it!"

Having little idea of how many had gathered to watch, I almost jumped a foot in the air. The deck felt alive beneath my paws, such was the outcry; feet were stamping, hands were clapping, men were cheering and whooping, buckets were being clanged, mops and brooms rapped against the bulkheads.

I looked up to see a beaming Lieutenant Hett approaching. He was all done up in his whites — he must have just returned from a shore trip — with his cap tucked under his arm so he could clap me as well.

Then he did something odd. He stopped right there in front of me, clicked his heels sharply and saluted me. "I officially promote you to the rank of able seaman," he told me, which caused a new round of cheers and applause to surge all around.

"Don't you mean able sea*cat*?" shouted someone. There was laughter.

Lieutenant Hett nodded. "Of course! I stand corrected. I hereby promote you to Able Seacat Simon. Ship's ratter of the highest order! Good for you!"

Then, before I had a chance to stop him, he picked the rat up by the tail, which drew another tumultuous cheer. I felt my heart swell. I had done it. I'd really *done* it.

"How about *that*, then?" Lieutenant Hett said, lifting the rat high in the air, where it swung, turning a circle, grey-brown, amorphous and limp.

And very dead.

"Farewell, Mao Tse-tung!" he said, and launched it into the river.

I watched the rat disappear and heard the "plunk" as it hit the water. A very satisfying "plunk" it was too. Though I was still breathing hard and knew my jaw would ache for hours, I don't think I could have felt happier if I'd tried.

But I didn't spend a great deal of time on celebrations. I was too exhausted. I went back to the captain's cabin, curled up on his bunk, and slept for some ten hours straight.

CHAPTER
SIXTEEN

The demise of the infamous and much hated rodent Mao Tse-tung brought about a marked lift in everyone's spirits. As for me, I couldn't have been more thrilled, particularly with my new name of Able Seacat Simon, which I delighted in hearing called out wherever I went. The next couple of weeks saw a general cheeriness even, reaching a particular high when the clever electricians managed to tune us into a programme on the radio which I was assured was a great favourite of everyone on board, being transmitted by something called the BBC.

I didn't know who or what the BBC was, but I didn't need to. It didn't last long, but there was laughter and chat and lots of singing, and — this *did* seem a miracle, especially when they said, "This one's for Flight Lieutenant Fearnley!" — it seemed much of the programme was dedicated to the crew of the *Amethyst*; something to cheer us up and to let everyone on board know that they hadn't been forgotten.

Which was precious. Because there was no doubt that, for all the peaks of jollity, the troughs of exhaustion and sadness and dejection were deep.

Most kept it hidden. Rather too well hidden, sometimes, I mused, so many of the sailors — particularly the ones who'd seen so much, suffered so much, had to tend to their dead and dying friends — feeling not quite able to articulate the shock and revulsion that I knew must regularly dance through their dreams. So I acted on what had now become a powerful instinct; I gave comfort where needed, in the shape of my physical presence and, increasingly, because sometimes the pain was buried deep, gave comfort where it wasn't even known that it was needed.

It was the strangest thing — well, at first. I soon learned to understand it. I'd have a rating pick me up, seemingly at random, and then they'd pull me close to their face — their conscious mind assuming that *they* were petting *me*. And then that outbreath. That sigh. That realisation seeping into them. That, actually, it was the other way around.

If the communist garrison leader — a Colonel Kang — hoped to break the crew, and have the captain agree to his terms, he had underestimated the strength of everyone's resolve. This was strengthened even further when, towards the end of June, three mail sacks got through to us, and better still came the news, following an otherwise fruitless meeting with Captain Kerans, that Kang was going to allow us to have delivered some of the reserves of fuel oil that were currently up in Nanking.

The captain, in a rare display of levity, almost clapped his hands together in glee. "Now that's what I call a mistake!" he told the officers. "I still can't quite believe it, I really can't."

"Perhaps there's been an instruction from on high, sir," Hett suggested. "You know. Humanitarian grounds and that. It won't look good if the men start dropping, will it?"

The captain scratched his head. I could see he was thinking about Kang. Though he'd not said it publicly, because he didn't want to frighten the men, I knew he believed everything Kang did was threatening. That he would have no compunction, if we crossed him, about killing us all. "Hmm, perhaps there has," he said. Then his face fell. "Or perhaps he's playing mind games again. I should have thought of that. We still have to *get* it."

It would be a long wait, too, but knowing it was coming, and that it would make everyone's lives so much more palatable in the increasing heat, raised everyone's spirits right up again. Then, ten days later, we greeted the day — a rare fine one — with the sight of a tug boat towing a lighter, approaching from upriver.

It took a while to be sure, but as it drew nearer, a cheer went up all over the *Amethyst*, as it became obvious that what it carried was the promised supply of oil. At last we'd have the means to light and ventilate the ship properly — simple things perhaps, but, in our current straits, *so* important.

Everyone free to do so crowded the starboard guardrails. The happy expectation turned out to be short-lived, however. As the craft tried to approach our

152

side, the tide had its own ideas about where the oil should be headed, thwarting every attempt to get alongside us, and pulling both tug and lighter away downstream.

There was no way it was going to get away without a fight, and, eventually, through the valiant efforts of the pilot (helped by Peggy, who barked encouragement throughout, possibly under the misapprehension that it held some dog food) the lighter was tied to us and the business of unloading it could begin. The only problem now — and it was a big one — was how that could be done. For all that the precious liquid was a godsend, every last drum of it, a little under three hundred drums would have to be hoisted on board and then drained into the oil fuel tank by hand.

But it was a challenge the men welcomed and they rolled their sleeves up willingly. They'd not had any decent exercise for some 82 days now, and everyone was feeling it. There was another wait first, because to do so at night would be too dangerous. With the dusk closing in, the captain decided "Operation Oil" would have to wait until the morning.

No one seemed to mind the dawn reveille, and it was cheering to hear the determination and commitment in the crew's voices as they began the mammoth task of transferring our welcome haul into the tank. It was a messy business; by lunch time there seemed to be oil everywhere. It was spilled on the decks, all over the crew and, less happily, up my nose — the smell of it being the nearest I decided I would like to get to it. It was hard enough to keep clean in the current conditions at the best of times, so I busied myself, as per usual, padding along all the still well-travelled rat runs, happy in the knowledge that the light and air and general lifting of spirits would help send the creatures back from where they came.

"To C in C," the captain said to Jack, when, by around four in the afternoon, the last drop was safely sloshing where it belonged. *"Fuel now on board. 54 tons. Operation commenced 05:00, finished at 16:00 hours, working nonstop throughout, 11 hours. They worked like TROJANS!"* he finished. "And make sure that's in capitals, Flags. What an excellent day's work."

There was further good news when a message arrived by boat a short while later in the form of a letter asking the captain to attend a meeting in Ching Kiang, the Communist People's Liberation Army's HQ, the following day.

"Might this be it, sir?" Hett asked him, as they gathered in the wireless room. "Might we finally be given permission to get away, do you think?"

"I hope so," said Captain Kerans. "Let's hope for the best, eh?"

But his expression told me the rest of what he was thinking. That at the same time, we should prepare for the worst.

The worst happened. Captain Kerans returned from the meeting stony-faced and sweating. Far from an agreement, he'd returned with yet another disappointment.

154

We might have oil, but they were still demanding an admission from the British Navy that not only had we fired first but that we shouldn't have even been there. That we had no right to be in Chinese waters in the first place, which was patently untrue. But as the communists were now controlling more and more territory around the Yangtse, their implacable stance held more and more sway.

There was even more; the captain had asked about replenishing our food stores, and was told in no uncertain terms that, as foreign merchant ships were no longer permitted to travel up the Yangtse, any ship — or plane — that attempted to go anywhere near the *Amethyst* would immediately be destroyed.

"And, of course, he reiterated his usual threat," the captain said gloomily. "The *Amethyst* will also be destroyed if we attempt to move it. So that's that. Another deadlock. I'm sorry to have to say so, but if we're going to play Kang at his own game, there's no choice. It's going to have to be half-rations from tomorrow."

The strain of our continued confinement was now making its presence felt right across the ship. Like the ensign that still flew above us, the crew — me included, because I was now on half-rations too — were getting droopy and ragged. Even Peggy was beginning to wilt — and she was usually immune to the extremes of temperature. I'd often catch her standing by a guardrail, looking wistfully at the sludge-coloured water below us. "She'll be in the river — you mark my words," Petty Officer Griffiths kept muttering. "She'll be in. For two pins, she'll be in, for a swim."

Still, Peggy, who managed to resist the temptation (just — I had no similar compunction) did what she could to cheer our friends up, as did I. But while we could curl up with our friends in the mess and watch them settle down to sleep, Captain Kerans increasingly seemed preoccupied and distant, mooching around on his own at all hours of the day and night.

It wasn't unexpected. After all, he'd been commanding a ship and crew in the most difficult and dispiriting conditions, and as the summer wore on the weather got even hotter, so keeping morale up among his young sailors must have been difficult.

With the daily grind being just that — a relentless and tedious round of mostly domestic drudgery — it was easy to forget the other spectre which still hung over the *Amethyst*: the fresh memories, there to stumble upon every time any of us passed over the quarterdeck — of the blood that had been shed and the lives that had been lost — of the friends we would never see again.

In the meantime, the game of what the captain had called "cat and mouse" with the garrison commander, Kang, was still showing no signs of being resolved. I didn't know which was which — who was the cat and who was the rodent? I hoped we weren't the latter — but it was obvious that the repeated to-ings and fro-ings, to attend yet more lengthy and up to now largely pointless-sounding meetings, were beginning to try the captain's patience to the utmost.

156

Either that, or he was doing what Jack had predicted we all might do before long, if we were stuck here much longer, and already "losing his marbles". I wasn't sure quite what that meant — couldn't even begin to guess at it — but, judging by Jack's expression when he'd said it, I suspected it wouldn't be a pretty sight.

Perhaps Captain Kerans had already lost them. Whenever it was warm and dry (an extremely rare and welcome combination) I had lately taken to returning to one of my old favourite high places — the glass-topped magnetic compass and gyro up on the bridge, which had miraculously survived the shelling unscathed. It was here, one afternoon a couple of days later, that I was to witness first hand evidence that Captain Kerans' "marbles" might have already deserted him.

"I need a detail of men mustered to deal with the blackout," he was telling Frank.

It was mid-July now, unbelievably. We'd been stuck here a whole two and a half months.

"The blackout?" Frank answered. He looked confused.

"Yes, it's not nearly good enough. Lights showing everywhere. We never seem sufficiently darkened at night. Something needs to be done about it."

Petty Officer Frank adjusted his face into a configuration I recognised. One that said, "*Really*, sir? You're *sure*, sir?" but without letting on.

"The blackout, sir," he said. "Something needs to be done?"

Captain Kerans flapped a hand. "Yes, it does. We need more blackout tarpaulins made. Particularly aft. Stern to amidships. Have a group of men run some up. Lots of them."

Frank's expression must have registered with Captain Kerans as well. Even with the oil, the power was still off by dusk. The nights couldn't be darker. He cleared his throat. "We need to keep the men *busy*, Frank. All this heat and lassitude is doing morale no good at all."

"Aye aye, sir," said Frank. "Excellent idea for the morale, sir." He bent his head to make a note of the instruction in his book.

"And we need to reduce topweight. The ship's very unstable. We need to strip down anything we can from the decks, particularly the upper decks — including removing some of the masts." He stopped then, perhaps noticing Frank's look of increasing consternation. "They can be stored below," he added. "Again, it's all work that will keep the men busy, Frank — stop them thinking quite so much about their empty stomachs."

"Aye, aye, sir," said Frank, once again scribbling furiously.

"And another thing," said the captain. "The anchor."

"Sir? The anchor?"

"The anchor, sir?" echoed an equally bemused-looking Lieutenant Hett, who'd just joined them.

"Yes, *specifically* the anchor chain," Captain Kerans repeated, looking like a man not to be messed with. "It needs a ruddy good greasing. Clangs about all the time

158

— specially on these high tides. Makes one hell of a racket. Driving me mad, it is. And it's only going to get worse if that typhoon comes along."

He was talking about Typhoon Gloria, a storm that had been building, that Jack had already told me might be headed our way. I'd never seen a typhoon before but felt strangely unafraid of it. With so much on our plates already — not least so much to be afraid of — a typhoon, sent by Mother Nature, seemed quite a benign thing. At least it might help stir things up a bit.

"The anchor chain, sir," Frank repeated, scribbling again. "Have it greased."

"Yes, a good quantity of grease and soft soap," the captain said. "That should do the job, I think. Oh, and while they're at it, have them wrap it well in bedding. Decent amount of blankets. That should do it. Stop the ruddy thing clanking away and getting on my nerves."

Lieutenant Hett said nothing this time, but I caught him raising his eyebrows while the captain wasn't looking, his attention still on the errant anchor chain.

"That's all, sir?" asked Frank.

"For the moment," said the captain. "And as soon as possible," he added. "Okay, Frank? That'll be all. As you were."

Captain Kerans stood and watched Hett and Frank walk away and down the ladder to the quarterdeck. He was looking very thin, and I wondered if he was eating his rations. Since I'd got to know him, I'd come to realise the sort of man he was, and I wouldn't have put it past him to have his own food distributed elsewhere.

And it was then that he looked up and saw me. "Ah, there you are, Able Seacat Simon!" he said, grinning up at me. Then he tapped his nose. "Ah," he said, mysteriously. "Walls have ears, Simon, my lad. That's the thing you must remember. Walls have ears."

I stared back down at him, every bit as confused as his officers. Walls had ears? Perhaps Jack had been right about the marbles.

CHAPTER
SEVENTEEN

The 30th July 1949, a day that would prove to be unlike any other, dawned hot and humid, as per usual. The only difference to be seen and felt was the effect of Typhoon Gloria. Though she'd not quite made a visit, she had come pretty close, the result of which was a high tide and fast-flowing current, and flooding on both banks of the river.

Gloria had certainly made herself felt over the previous week, and in our already difficult straits had added another set of problems. The top of the ship had to be stripped of anything that might be blown away — all the canvas the men had been busy assembling and hanging at the captain's orders, plus the covers over the guns, and all the other awnings. Then it was simply a case of waiting and hoping. As the wind rose and rose, most of us huddled under some sort of cover — at least grateful for the marked dip in temperature — till the worst of it blew itself out.

Not that it had all been doom and gloom. And, as I'd suspected, it had certainly stirred things up a bit. Just after the worst of the wind passed, there was suddenly a great commotion — Peggy, who I'd thought had been dozing in Petty Officer Griffiths' cabin, was out on deck, barking herself hoarse.

We all went out to find out what was going on, gathering at the guardrails, to see a haystack floating past the *Amethyst*, with a dog standing on top of it, barking back. Peggy was beside herself, understandably. Was this the first fellow canine she'd seen in a year? Probably. I wondered if we'd see a cat next.

"Shall we try to lasso it for you, Pegs?" Petty Officer Griffiths was saying to her, laughing.

"I think it's love at first sight," remarked Lieutenant Strain drily.

There was more to come. Soon another haystack appeared in the distance, this one topped off not by a cat, but by a chicken.

"Ruddy hell, is this some evil communist torture?" Frank said. "God, what I wouldn't give to see that roasted on a plate."

But if the chicken had roused the crew's hunger, the next thing had them drooling — for it was not a haystack this time, but a pig!

"Saints alive," somebody shouted from above me. "Someone fetch some rope or something! Anything! We can get that! A whole *pig*!"

There was a frantic scrabble while everyone flew in all directions, trying to find something to lasso the animal with before the tide pulled it out of our reach. And they made a good fist of it; more than once managing to get a rope round it before the current got the upper hand and the pig, looking up at its

162

tormentors with terrified eyes, managed to slip the makeshift noose.

"No fresh pork for dinner tonight, then," Frank observed, as it disappeared into the distance and whatever alternative fate awaited it. "Bully beef it is, then," he added, sighing, and as I looked at the men's expressions, the brief excitement snatched from them — literally — I couldn't help but wish they liked sardines as much as I did. For all the privations, we had more than enough of those.

"Woof," said Peggy, dolefully. We all knew how she felt.

Though the effects of Typhoon Gloria were largely behind us now, we had much to be grateful to her for. We didn't know it yet, but the high tide, the current and the flooding on the banks were all going to be our friends.

However, when I entered Captain Kerans' cabin that afternoon, in the interests of giving him some moral support, I had no idea quite how much Gloria was going to mean to us, and how soon.

There was no getting away from it; conditions were deteriorating rapidly. I had come from the wireless room — no longer a warm cosy spot but a raging cauldron — so much so that poor Jack was barely able to think straight from heat exhaustion. Junior ratings were taking turns to sit with him and pump a pair of the ship's bellows over him, but he was in such a bad way now that he sometimes struggled to write, let alone try to decode incoming messages — of which, over the last few days there seemed to have been many.

There were also mutterings all over the ship — mutterings the captain had been at pains to quell — about what was going to happen once this new oil ran out, which it soon would, even with the ship being powered down at night. And what about the food? We were almost out of flour, the sugar was spoiled now, the rats — growing fatter on it — were breeding unchecked.

The flooding hadn't helped, either. Because of it, communication with the shore had been impossible, so such supplies as we'd been able to trade for were no longer available to us.

No, all in all, things were not looking good for the *Amethyst*, and as I caught the captain's eye once inside his cabin, I could tell he was thinking about that too; about just how far the communists intended to push us. To the death? Then, with a thrill of excitement, I saw something else twinkling in his eyes. Did he know something no one else did?

I settled myself down in my usual spot, just beside the typewriter on which he bashed out his reports. But it seemed that he hadn't been writing, but drawing. He picked up the result of his efforts — a pencil sketch of a ship — and hung it from his fingers in front of me.

"Shall I tell you a secret, Simon?" he said.

Galvanised and rapt now, I stood up and stretched, then resettled and made myself more comfortable. I was glad I had, because it turned out to be quite a big secret. And also an explanation for all the strange goings-on that almost the entire crew had been muttering and moaning about these past couple of weeks. The business of the greasing and blanketing of the anchor. The business of the *Amethyst* being shrouded in sheets. The business of taking down all that metal topweight and slinging it unceremoniously overboard or below. The business of still being so frugal with the oil.

He wasn't losing his marbles. He had had all his wits about him. He was setting things in place to try to silence and disguise the *Amethyst*. He was preparing for us all to escape!

"What we're going to do," he confirmed, to my great excitement, "is make a dash for it. Tonight. Yes, I know it's dangerous, but there's no need to look at me like that, Simon. I promise you, I have thought all this through. For weeks, let me tell you. We're going to make a break for it under cover of darkness later this evening. Look. See this here?"

He pointed to where he'd done some shading with his pencil. "I'm going to disguise the *Amethyst* — well, to the extent that I can do, at any rate — disguise her enough to at least give those communists pause for thought. To be uncertain that they are looking at what they think they are looking at. And then we are going to escape."

There was no hesitation. No judicious use of the word "try". We are *going to* escape. So the men had been wrong in their mutterings and chunterings. Captain Kerans had pulled the wool right over their eyes.

Having already told Williams, the chief engineer, earlier in the day, so he would have time to raise steam in the boilers, Captain Kerans gave Frank a list of names. He was to inform everyone on the list — all the chief petty officers and petty officers — to assemble in his cabin, plus a number of the senior ratings, all of them maintaining utmost security at all times.

It was early evening when they arrived, the sky outside turning a darkening peachy pink, and the temperature still as warm as it had been all day. So with some seventeen men crammed into the tiny airless space, it was something of a hot, uncomfortable squeeze. I didn't mind, though. I was too excited about everything to want to be anywhere else, so I settled again, just by the voice pipe to the wheelhouse, keen to listen in on his briefing.

"I have decided to make a break for it tonight," he told everyone. "Now, I know it's not going to be easy without a pilot to guide us, but the darkness is going to help us — the moon sets just after 23:00. And it won't be as good for another month after tonight. The river's high because of the typhoon, too, which should give us some advantage, and we need to slip at 22:00." He paused to let this sink in. "That's crucial if we're going to pass the big guns at Woosung before dawn. I don't doubt that if they are on to us, that's where we're going to get it. So speed," he glanced over at Williams, "is going to be of the very essence."

There was silence for a moment as the officers took this in, then the mood changed and they all began bombarding him with questions — every one of which he seemed to have an answer for. He really *had* been thinking about this for a long time, I realised. No wonder he'd seemed so preoccupied.

They soon dispersed — because now time *was* very much of the essence — and everyone had a precise role to play to make Captain Kerans' dream of escape a reality. There was no room for doubt. This was our only chance of making a run for it, and there wasn't a man there, I think, who didn't want to take it.

Frank grinned at me, then, having saluted the captain, as if on an impulse, scooped me up and tucked me under his arm. I wondered if — perhaps given what had happened the last time — he intended to take me down to the wheelhouse to bring him luck.

"You hear that?" he said. "Finally, it's happening! You know what we're going to do, Blackie boy? No? Well, I'll tell you. We're going to give that ruddy Kang a right smack in the eye!"

After so long being trapped, I felt the same excitement everyone else did. I just hoped Kang wouldn't slap us right back.

CHAPTER
EIGHTEEN

Yangtse River, 22:09 hours, 30 July 1949

Despite knowing what was happening, and by now having every faith in Captain Kerans' ability to *make* it happen, in that hour or so remaining before we were going to make the dash for it, I started feeling frightened again. I couldn't seem to help it. It just crept up on me, like the mosquitoes would creep up on the sleeping sailors. It wasn't too bad at first; just a feeling that I couldn't quite articulate, nothing more tangible than a vague sense of unease. But when I walked across the deck, close to the X guns, and caught the distinctive whiff of their recent oiling on the damp evening air, that's when it properly hit me.

A memory pounced on me then — a memory that wasn't even quite a memory. I remembered so little of the actual attack. Remembered almost nothing of those minutes in any detail — but the sound and smell of the guns had never quite left me, any more than had the sight of all the bodies. Though I'd become long used to seeing all the shell holes and twisted metal around the ship — and that emblematic battered ensign — the thought of the guns being manned and fired again tonight was more than enough to have the sensations flooding back. All at once, I felt ambushed by a powerful, mortal fear, and it was an act of will to force it out of my mind.

I knew many of the crew must feel the same. Over the months of our captivity, no matter how much they tried to push the memories down, many of them had relived the events of that day constantly; had kept seeing again the things they wished they hadn't had to see in the first place. And I wasn't surprised, because so many of them were still young and inexperienced. Like gentle George, who'd found me, so few of them had seen the brutal reality of war before this — even fewer, I suspected, had ever seen death. So I understood how frightened they must now be feeling again. And they knew I would always keep their confidences, too; keep those memories of the private tears some had shed to myself.

"There is no courage without fear." I remembered Captain Skinner saying that to me. And he was right. You didn't need to be brave if you weren't afraid. A part of me felt a welcome kernel of excitement growing inside me at the sheer courage — the audacity — of what we were about to try to do. As I took up my position close to Captain Kerans (which thankfully nobody seemed to object to, even if Peggy, Queen of Incessant Barking, had been shut up down in the sick berth, just to be on the safe side) I realised I felt ready for anything, despite the constant undercurrent of fear.

The final couple of hours had not been without incident. The captain had gone up to the bridge before

169

eight, keen to get his eyes used to the dark well before the time came to raise the anchor. Despite the advantages of the high tide and flooding, the Yangtse was still a dangerous river, and as we were without either a pilot or any charts now, being able to see with the naked eye was crucial.

And what he'd seen had been a sampan in the distance, that was heading our way.

Having been unable to get to us for over a week, due to Gloria, the traders who sold us produce (by now at ridiculously inflated prices) had, tonight of all nights, decided to make the crossing. With everyone now ready to go, and the evidence clear all over the *Amethyst*, there was a moment of panic about what should be done.

The captain thought on his feet. "On no account let them board," he told Lieutenant Hett. "And have some camp beds set up on the quarterdeck. Have some men get in them, as if they're turning in. We must make it look as if everything is normal. Get some goods. Check the invoice. Act completely normally."

And everyone did. But there couldn't have been a crew member on board who wasn't holding his breath. If news got passed on to Kang of even the tiniest oddity, our imminent deaths were now staring us in the face.

"Lord, it's dark," the captain observed, peering out into the inky night through his binoculars, the traders having thankfully left again. Despite his eyes having "adjusted", that was the thing with humans; they really

170

couldn't see much after nightfall, which I supposed was why they tended to go to sleep. But not tonight, and the captain's determination to free us only increased my respect for him further. It was a truly courageous decision to do the thing he was about to do, and I knew I must take my lead from him.

I also couldn't help but remember what Colonel Kang had told him every single time they'd spoken: that "if you move your ship, every attempt will be made to destroy it. If you do not, all will be well."

All *would* be well. We were going anyway, *despite* him and his threats, and all would *still* be well. We were going to slip and turn the *Amethyst* as soon as the moon nudged behind a convenient cloud, so I wrapped my tail around my paws and peered downriver alongside the captain and Lieutenant Hett, wishing I could reassure them on that point. For, much as I believed it, that wasn't the case, at least not as yet.

There really wasn't much to see, even with my excellent vision. Just the oily, lapping blackness of the river, the silhouetted shores — raggy and lace-like against the moonlit night sky — and the odd moth and winged beetle, flying low over the water, and — *hang on!* I craned my neck further. Wait — I *could* see something!

And so, evidently, could the captain. "Good Lord!" he said to Hett, who was also peering through his binoculars. "See that, Number One? It's only another ship! What the devil?"

They both lowered their binoculars, then raised them again. "Seems we have our pilot after all, eh?" said the captain. Then he leaned towards the voice pipe to his right. "Slow ahead port engines," he commanded, his voice taut with tension. "Wheel amidships. Black smoke." The *Amethyst* responded. We were finally underway.

Everyone seemed to hold their breath at that point, it seeming a miracle that we could ever be so lucky. Because the presence of this other vessel was good news indeed. The captain's biggest concern — which he had voiced only an hour earlier — was whether a big frigate such as the *Amethyst* would be able to safely negotiate the deep water channel in the middle of the river without a pilot. One slip-up and we could so easily run aground on the bank again. So the arrival of this other ship — which was strung with lights, and soon identified as a merchant ship called the *Kiang Ling Liberation* — felt like the best omen possible.

"Five degrees starboard," Captain Kerans ordered, his binoculars following the merchant ship. "We'll drop astern of her and follow her through instead."

This was it, I realised, my whole body tensed in anticipation. After all these long weeks in captivity, we were finally doing it! We were making our escape!

Or, at least, trying to. Every second seemed to pass agonisingly slowly as inch by inch the *Amethyst* moved through the dark water. With our smoke belching aft now, the night felt even darker, the river's shores blacker mounds in the distance. No one on the bridge said a word, but I knew every last man on board was silently waiting for the same thing to happen; for the moment when the communists saw us and began blasting us out of the water. Destroying us, just as they'd promised they would.

But it seemed the blanketed anchor and greased chain had done the job the captain wanted, and as we began to slice along behind the Chinese merchant vessel, the blackout sheeting seemed to be doing its job too, evidently making the *Amethyst* all but invisible to the batteries, just as Captain Kerans had hoped it would.

No such luck for the *Kiang Ling Liberation*. No sooner had we slipped alongside her, hidden now from view, than the shore was suddenly alive with activity.

"They're firing!" the captain shouted, above the roar of shell fire and machine guns. "They're firing at *her*! What the devil?"

And it seemed they were. The big merchant ship, already lit by its gay strings of lightbulbs, was now even more ablaze — with orange licks of leaping, murderous flame.

"What the *devil?*" the captain said again, his binoculars at his face again. "You see that, Hett? What the devil's going on over there?"

I stood transfixed; paralysed now, both with fear and consternation, hearing distant shouts and cries as the *Kiang Ling*'s crew ran for cover; as the shells pounded against her, above and around her. Yet still we moved, following the same line as the stricken, flaming vessel. A minute passed. Five minutes. Ten minutes. More. Until she slowed, fully ablaze now, and we began to nose ahead of her, away from the batteries, away from Kang, away from the shells and the bullets, incredibly, astoundingly, unbelievably unscathed.

"Looks like we've got away with it so far," said Lieutenant Strain. He sounded as stunned as everyone felt.

Captain Kerans raised his binoculars again, peering back from where we'd come. The merchant ship seemed to have been run aground now, as well. "Yes," he conceded, "it does indeed, doesn't it?" He lowered his binoculars, and his expression was at odds with the calm way he'd spoken. "Those gunners on the shore must have been asleep."

But even as he said it, the words were true no longer. No sooner had he finished speaking than new explosions broke the stillness, and the sky above the *Amethyst* was alive with flares.

"Hard astern!" ordered the captain. "Perhaps we haven't got away with it after all. It looks like there's a patrol boat coming to meet us!"

But then something else inexplicable happened — it began firing not on *us*, but at the shore battery that had sent all the flares up — which made no sense at all. Had the darkness and disguise really confused them *that* much?

"Well I never!" exclaimed Hett, newly stunned. "What's all *that* about?"

"Not an earthly," the captain admitted, as the shore battery returned their fire. "B gun, open fire! Might as well add to the confusion, eh?"

By now it seemed nothing was making sense. I jumped down from my station on top of the electrical box, and prudently took up a lower one below it. Keen as I had been to see as much as I could of the action, the words "sitting duck" were now again fresh in my mind, and as the fizzing balls of light winged their way over and around us, I felt glad of the protection and security of the bulkhead. As my paws hit the corticene, I realised I was shaking all over. Was the captain shaking too? Was Lieutenant Hett? Lieutenant Strain?

If they'd not been up before then, then they certainly were now. No sooner had we passed the smoking hulk of the Chinese merchant ship than an enormous explosion at the bow of the *Amethyst* almost knocked all three officers off their feet.

The captain grabbed the windscreen and regained his balance. "They've found us!" he barked then, to the voice pipe, to Jack. "Message to C in C. I am under heavy fire and have been hit!" He then sent orders for our remaining four-inch gun to open fire, and moments later, I knew from the reassuring vibration beneath my belly, that we were now travelling down the Yangtse at full speed. More than full speed, in fact. A whopping 22 knots, according to the engine room — faster than the *Amethyst* was supposed to even be capable of. But like a cat with a dog on its tail, she gave her all. She really was running for her life — and for ours — after almost three and a half months of captivity.

Not that it was plain sailing from then on. We sailed down-river without incident till long after midnight (Captain Kerans even found time to pull me from my safe place and reassure me, presumably thinking I was a great deal more stressed than I was by this time). Then, on approaching the shore batteries at Kiang Yin at 01:00 hours, he realised another substantial obstacle lay in our way: the make-shift defensive boom the communists had stretched across this part of the river, made up, the captain explained to Lieutenant Hett, from sunken merchant ships from an earlier war. Almost impossible to make out in the darkness, bar a few broken masts, it only allowed safe passage though a narrow stretch midstream.

We approached the boom, the *Amethyst* a deeper dark within the dappled dark of moonlight. It soon became clear that the passage — which would normally be marked on either side by guide lights — would not be very safe to negotiate after all, as only one of the two lights was lit.

There was a tense silence as the officers strained to make out some detail in the blackness that might help guide the ship through the channel. "Port or starboard?" asked the captain finally. "Which way do you think, Number One?"

Hett shook his head. "I really wouldn't like to say, sir."

It was soon clear that we also weren't alone on the river. Not that we'd expected to be. The captain knew that the communists upriver almost certainly would have alerted their comrades by now that the *Amethyst* had eluded them and was on her way. And it seemed they had, because a patrol boat was already speeding out to meet us, opening fire with tracer shells as it ploughed through the dark water.

I don't think there could have been a man or beast on board who wasn't once again holding their breath as we neared the boom. I thought once again of my mother, and how she'd told me that, sometimes, all you have to fall back on is instinct; a voice inside which you must listen to very carefully.

I looked across at the captain, and I could see him doing exactly that; trying to conjure up the instinct that would tell him what to do to preserve the safety of his ship and the lives of his men.

"Five degrees port!" he said at last, his voice strong and decisive, and, as we watched and waited for the sickening crump of metal that would mean he'd made the wrong choice, it was as if time had slowed down to an agonising crawl.

But he hadn't made the wrong choice. The single light slid silently by us and, though I doubt they really did, given the still precarious nature of our bid for freedom, I felt sure I could hear the men cheering below.

"We're not out of the woods yet, Simon," Captain Kerans was quick to warn me, as I leaped back up onto the electrical box in order to resume moral support. "Bridge to wheel-house," he said, "Woosung — what time are we likely to get there?"

"Around 03:00 hours, sir," came Frank's voice up the voice pipe, "barring any more unforeseen incidents. Though I doubt we'll get past without some sort of response from them, do you?"

The captain didn't really need to answer.

★ ★ ★

There was one unforeseen incident, just before the fort at Woosung was reached. We were travelling fast — still as fast as the *Amethyst* could manage — the same full, and — barring gunfire — unstoppable 22 knots. The Chinese junk that suddenly loomed in front of our bows was no match for us, and left little room to take avoiding action. The smaller boat was sliced clean in half.

There was no time to wonder if the crew had leaped to safety, as almost as soon as we'd left the junk's debris in our wake, the fort's searchlights began dancing on the water.

"Here we go . . ." observed Lieutenant Strain, his profile grim as he raised his binoculars. "If they didn't know then they must *surely* know now. If we're for it, this is where we're going to cop it."

But then a curious thing happened. Though the searchlights repeatedly found us, not a single shore gun opened fire, not even when one of the lights caught us in its beam and rested on the ship for almost half a minute.

"Well, I'll be jiggered," said Hett, as the light slid away again.

"What on earth's going on?" wondered Fearnley, who'd now joined us on the bridge.

"Do you know what, men?" Captain Kerans said, lowering his binoculars. "I think they've had enough. I think they're *actively* letting us pass."

"*Really*, sir?" asked Hett, voicing exactly my question. After the way they'd attacked before, it seemed hard to believe.

178

"I do," he said, visibly beginning to relax now, as the lights of the fort began sliding back astern. "I wonder if perhaps they feel well rid of us, don't you, Number One? Yes, I think that might be it. In fact, I'm sure I'm correct," he finished. "I suspect Mao Tse-tung is *very* glad to see the back of us."

There was a sound from below. A familiar one, too. A distinct "woof!". Peggy obviously agreed.

PART THREE

PART THREE

CHAPTER
NINETEEN

We were united with the fleet — well, our friends on HMS *Consort*, who'd come steaming along to greet us — just as we cleared the river's estuary. Now it really was time for congratulations and celebrations. We'd spent a full 101 days trapped up the Yangtse, and we were finally back on the open ocean.

As soon as we were free — and, oh, how glorious it was to be out on the open sea again! — Captain Kerans had Jack send a message. "Have rejoined the fleet south of Woosung. No damage or casualties. God save The King."

And The King, to the delight of everyone on board, signalled back.

"Please convey to the commanding officer and ship's company of HMS *Amethyst* my hearty congratulations on their daring exploit to rejoin the fleet. The courage, skill and determination shown by all on board have my highest commendation. Splice the mainbrace."

Needless to say, everyone did.

The next twenty-four hours passed in something of a blur. The *Concord* came alongside us and resupplied us with much-needed oil, and then, soon after dark, we were joined by another ship, the *Jamaica*, which was carrying all our mail — this had the men almost beside themselves with excitement. There was also a band, who were out on deck and playing for us, as she steamed all around us, a tune Frank said was called "Rolling down the River".

"Not that we had much chance to do any rolling!" he pointed out to Petty Officer Griffiths as we watched them from the quarterdeck. "Rolling? No ruddy time for any of that!"

There was no time for anything much at all now, as in a little over two days we'd be docked in Hong Kong, the ordeal finally over, where we'd been warned that there was "one hell of a reception" waiting for us, as the captain put it.

I wasn't sure what "one hell of a reception" might feel like, but with the mood on board so buoyant, I was as swept up in the atmosphere as everyone else was. Had I a tail like Peggy's, I would have wagged it. As it was, I hadn't — my own tail "wagged" for rather different reasons — but I don't think I'd spent so much time purring in months.

"You know, young fellow," Captain Kerans said, as we steamed towards home, "you're still so very young, but I reckon you've lived more lives than many cats do in their entire lifetimes!"

I thought I probably had, too.

And then, before I knew it, we were home. Gazing out towards the hills that rose steeply in the distance, I felt almost as if we'd never been away.

184

It was good to see Hong Kong again. Good to see the sheer, happy bustle of it. Good to see the sampans bobbing in the bay, their brightly coloured sails like the wings of so many butterflies, all of which had chosen this perfect shimmering bay on which to settle.

Approaching the docks, I was also pleased — if a little overwhelmed — to see the thousands of people who had come out to welcome us back.

In truth, I found it difficult to believe what I was seeing. Despite there having been many signals back and forth to prepare us for the escort we'd be receiving — and for the throng that would likely be greeting us — the sight of all the sailors lining the decks of the escort convoy was quite astonishing. Even more astonishing was the sheer volume of the cheers and whoops and whistles that kept ringing out, again and again, across the bay.

Peggy, true to form, was like an animal possessed. Had it not been so firmly attached to the rest of her, her tail would have been in danger of becoming detached. As it was, she was kept from getting too over-excited by a makeshift leash tied around her neck, which seemed to be fashioned from a length of sailmaker's twine. At least it kept her from leaping bodily into the water at the dockside, which had been suggested several times as a strong possibility. It also silenced her to an extent, because she couldn't seem to understand that if she strained too hard against it, it prevented her from barking, so she kept trying to do both at once.

Watching her doing this, I was very glad no one considered me enough of a nuisance to put such a contraption round *my* neck. Though, once I thought about it, if they *had* got such an idea into their heads, I'd have probably "skedaddled", just like George used to, before they even tried.

I felt very much like skedaddling, in any case, if I was honest, because the closer we got to our berth at the dockside the more the press of people began to alarm me. So much shouting, so much waving, such a huge number of people, adding an extra layer of anxiety to that which was already welling, at the fire crackers and hooters that kept going off and making me jump.

Not that I would be given much chance to escape, because while the ship was being oiled, resupplied and fixed up as much as was necessary, there was a certain naval function Peggy and I had been told we must attend.

"You are the hero of the hour!" Captain Kerans announced a few days after we'd docked. "You and Peggy both, but particularly you, it seems, Simon. And guess what. You are not only going to be awarded an *Amethyst* Campaign Medal, you are going to get another medal too!"

He was sitting in his cabin, with Lieutenant Hett and Lieutenant Berger. Berger had rejoined the ship after our escape, having recovered from the wounds he'd suffered back in April.

The captain was half hidden under mountains of paperwork. It had been the same since we'd docked. All sorts of paperwork had been delivered, to replace all the charts and documents Lieutenant Weston had had to burn, I supposed, as well as all sorts of official-looking files.

He flapped a piece of paper he held in one hand, and patted his knee with the other. I didn't need to jump, though, because Lieutenant Hett scooped me up and plonked me on the captain's lap.

"Now then, see this?" he told me. "This is a letter of confirmation that you are to be officially awarded the Dickin Medal, which is a decoration awarded to only the bravest and most courageous animals, who have helped their human friends in times of war. And there's more — you are the very first cat ever to be awarded one. How about that? How about *that?*" he repeated to the other men. "I had no idea about that, did you?" Both shook their heads. "Pigeons, dogs, horses, but *never* a cat. Quite something, eh?" He turned back to me, his eyes bright. He seemed amused by it all. "And now a cat has been awarded one. *You,* Simon." He looked pretty pleased with himself, I decided. "You are going to be decorated *twice!* At the Royal Navy Fleet Club, tomorrow night, as it happens."

"*If* we manage to get him there," Lieutenant Hett pointed out.

"Shall I have Dusty see if he can rustle up a crate for us?" asked Lieutenant Berger. "We can't risk carrying him down there, can we?"

The captain shook his head. "No, we can't. Good idea. Or a strong cardboard box. See what he can come up with. Anyway, how about that, Simon? The hero of the hour!" he looked more than pleased. He looked delighted.

"Or a trunk," Lieutenant Hett was saying. A *trunk*? I was alarmed now. "We could always pop him in a trunk. And if we put a lead on him, just in case . . ."

A *lead*? I was not liking this one little bit.

"And you can be sure there'll be a hullaballoo once this hits the press," the captain added. "They're sending a collar for him as well, by all accounts. That's for you to wear in lieu of the medal, Simon," he explained to me. "Then, when we return to England you'll be presented with the medal itself — in London. Bit of pomp and circumstance for you to enjoy!"

He still looked delighted. He couldn't have looked *more* delighted. But all this talk of collars and hullaballoos was beginning to make me anxious. Not to mention trunks and leads and strong cardboard boxes. And presentations at fleet clubs, whatever they were. It all sounded very, very worrying to me.

I decided that a course of evasive action would be necessary. They would have to have their presentation without me. I made myself scarce. For two days.

We were just over a month in Hong Kong. The *Amethyst* was restocked with supplies and refuelled, and such repairs that were immediately necessary were completed, and such hullaballoos as were deemed necessary were also completed, all of which I tried to give an equally wide berth.

Not so my shipmates, who seemed to revel in their new status as heroes, and deservedly so. It was only now, with them safe and rested, that I think I truly realised how much of a toll the whole experience had taken.

Everyone had been given leave, and they were making the most of it, allowing me to see them in a very different and welcome light. Now our ordeal was over, they seemed energised; bright-eyed and smiling. To an extent it was as if they'd been reborn — as if they too had nine lives and, having just lost one, were determined to plunge enthusiastically into the next.

So, while I kept to my routines (the *Amethyst* might be berthed, but there were still rats that needed hunting) my friends came and went, often seeming almost as over-excited as Peggy. I was reminded of the tottering revellers I used to observe at night back when I was still a kitten, sitting on an oil drum or pile of pallets in the moonlight, more often than not mystified by all the strange activities.

Now I studied my friends' antics from up on the bridge, where I still stood watch for at least some portion of the night, my view of them so different now, and in such an unexpected way.

What a long way we'd all come together.

Though I'd had no particular desire to leave the ship during our time in Hong Kong, on our last day in dock I had a sudden change of heart. It suddenly struck me we'd be sailing for England in a matter of hours.

I knew everything and nothing about this fabled place called England. I knew it was home for most of my friends, that it was always spoken of with love and reverence, and that the men seemed to almost ache for it, so keen were they to see it again. But I also knew it was far away — far further than I'd ever been — and in the north, where it was apparently often cold; a kind of cold I'd been told I would've "never known the likes of" and which, in the oppressive heat of a Yangtse night, my friends would yearn for.

I had no such yearning. I didn't see why anyone would like the cold. As with being "wet through", which had turned out to be decidedly unpleasant, I suspected I wouldn't like "cold" one little bit. But as all I wanted was to stay on the *Amethyst*, I was happy enough. I would go where she went; where my friends went.

It did occur to me that with England being so far away, it might be a very long time before I saw Hong Kong again. Who knew? I might never come back here. In thinking that, I felt a sudden powerful urge to say goodbye to it. To sit, for a while, on the end of the jetty. To be close, for just a short time, to my mother. So while everyone was busy with the last of the preparations I slipped away down the gangway onto the dock I hadn't set my paws on for well over a year.

It was the strangest thing. I remembered the way. All that time away at sea — all those adventures, all those trials, all those lives I'd been living — and yet it wasn't even as if I had to consciously remember. It was the opposite. It was as if I'd never been away.

I padded away from the quay, feeling unexpected waves of nostalgia and sadness come over me. Having been away so long, I soon realised just how much I'd forgotten, from the sight of my beloved banyans and the caws of the cockatoos, to the green softness of the hills that rose up beyond the city, as if hugging it in their protective embrace. Particularly intense was the feel of sand and earth beneath my paws, both so unexpectedly soft and warm and fragrant after the cold unyielding corticene I'd grown so used to. But I also understood why my senses had forgotten them. Because that was what being a cat was all about. We thrived because we knew how to live where we were, rather than — as humans often seemed to, I'd discovered — where our hearts wished to be.

Not that I wished to be anywhere but the *Amethyst* now, living with the friends who had become so precious to me. As I left the bustle of the harbour, the feeling only intensified, as every new vista pulled me back to some wisp of painful memory that reminded me how lucky I'd been. Not in losing my mother, whose presence I still felt constantly, but to have escaped from the miseries of those last months as a stray, when I'd hunt till my pads were raw, getting drenched and despondent, and sit at the end of the jetty and wonder what kind of better life there might be beyond the bay.

I felt proud that I'd found the courage to go in search of it — well, once the terror had abated, anyway. That I'd allowed myself to be scooped up by dear sweet Ordinary Seaman George Hickinbottom — where was he now, I wondered? — who I missed still. He would never know how grateful I was that he'd given me the opportunity to live a life I could never have imagined. To become the cat I could never have imagined either.

It was a warm morning, the rain that had greeted our arrival having cleared, and as I padded along the familiar tracks and pathways, alternately bright and shady under the tamarinds and banyans, I let the happier memories of that earlier time wash over me.

Memories of the kind old lady who used to live in the big house — which I now hurried past automatically, slightly braced, automatically fearful — the hunting forays (how proud I hoped Mum would now be of me!), the anxious crossings of the murderous road that spilt the island into two, and our little jetty on the far shore. This stood exactly as I'd left it — reaching out from the sand, gnarly plank by gnarly plank, on past the shingle, to hover above the water as if a path to something wonderful, where we'd sit and gaze up at the moon.

There was no moon now. The sky, the same intense butterfly-wing blue I would always remember, was reflected in the gently lapping water, which in turn was sprinkled, as it always was, with shards of dancing sunshine. Almost on an impulse, I jumped down onto the sand and slipped beneath the jetty, aware as I did so how much bigger I'd grown, how much smaller our sometime home seemed. *Small and safe, kitten.* I could almost hear my mother saying it.

I spent a few moments there, luxuriating in the welcome cool and shade, remembering what I'd left here, idly following the progress of a tiny lizard between

192

the pebbles, but feeling not even the tiniest urge to stretch a paw out and toy with it.

My mother had been right. It had been my safe place and I was glad I'd come back; it felt good to return here and experience it again. But it wasn't long before I felt the tug of the *Amethyst* calling me back to her. And, perhaps, floating on the breeze, the sound of Peggy, too — yapping furiously about nothing in particular, as she so often did, and Coxswain Frank, hollering irritably from some corner of the ship or other, "Will someone *please* shut that ruddy dog up!"

I didn't linger longer. It was time to head back. To my new life, my dear friends, to my quarters — which were admittedly various. And some of them perhaps a little too fine for a working naval seacat. But then, as Jack had pointed out, I was "decorated now", wasn't I? It still felt slightly unreal, that, and it humbled me to even think about it, but I was reassured that we'd be back at sea soon and all the fuss would die down. (Captain Kerans had reassured me, when all the people had swarmed so alarmingly up the gangway, my "fan-club", whatever that was, definitely couldn't come with us *there*.)

As I left the shore, a flock of cockatoos took flight, as if to wish me well. Time to say goodbye to Hong Kong. Time to go home.

CHAPTER
TWENTY

My absence had caused something of a commotion. I wasn't aware of it at first, because the *Amethyst* looked exactly as she had when I'd left her, bar the one difference I welcomed — that all the well-wishers seemed to have left. The sun was strong on my back now, and the long walk had left me feeling weary. I realised it was the first time I'd travelled such a distance in over a year, and my hind legs were busy reminding me.

But all was not as I'd left it, clearly, because before I'd so much as placed a paw on the gangway, a shout rang out from high above me, and I looked up to see Jack, waving his arms to someone down on the lower deck, shouting, "He's back! Martin! Paddy! Look! No, not that way — *that* way! Sid, get down there and grab him! Get him back! Take the herrings!" upon which there was a scramble to locate the fish they'd obviously found for me, in the hopes — or so I assumed — that I might need some enticement to be coaxed back on board again. As if there was a chance that I might decide *not* to board the ship again. As if they might need (and at this I was confused and confounded) to *persuade* me that my life and home was with them.

194

By the time I'd padded up the gangway, feeling grateful that the ship placed it in shadow — a balm for my much-too-hot paws — Sid and Martin were already crouched at the top of it, waiting, the legs of their shorts flapping and their caps pushed right back, a pair of hopeful grins on their faces. There was no sign of Jack, so I assumed he was still shimmying down to us. Somebody must have seen me leave the ship, I realised.

"C'mon, Blackie. That's the boy," said Martin, gesturing to the saucer on the deck in front of him. "Here you go. Fishy fishy! Some lovely herrings for you — look! Orders of the captain. Opened specially, they were. Just for you."

I duly went up and sniffed the fish, and Martin began to stroke me. "Where've you been, little fella?" he wanted to know. "Off to find your sweetheart? You've had us at sixes and sevens, you have, Blackie. Caused one almighty hulla-ballo, I can tell you. The boss has been beside himself — it was him saw you leave. Can you imagine the to-do if we sailed back to Blighty and the hero of the hour wasn't with us?"

I was beginning to feel increasingly humbled by all this, not to mention touched that the captain had spotted me leaving and set up a watch for my return. And guilty for having been the cause of yet another hullaballoo. Guilty too, about being called the "hero of the hour" — as if every man and man-boy aboard the *Amethyst*, not to mention those who'd been taken from us by the communists, were anything less than heroes themselves. Not forgetting Peggy, who, despite the misfortune of having been a dog (or perhaps because of it) didn't have a bad bone in her body, as Jack had once told me — well, not unless she'd eaten one, that was.

In any event, I was glad to be back amongst my friends again, and without so much as a whisker of regret in my head that we'd be off to sea again and might never be required to come back.

A whistle sounded, and it was only then that I realised that the ship must be weighing anchor sooner than I'd thought. Either that or the time had passed faster than I'd known. In any event, it made more sense of the panic at my arrival, and it also struck me (with only slightly less panic) that had I stayed longer on the beach I could have been too late. An image formed in my head then, of rounding the quay and seeing only sea and sky and sampans where the *Amethyst* should be. That's when it really hit me fully: I could have come back — *to* my home — and found it no longer there.

"Not hungry? Well, there's a first." It was Jack, who'd come down and joined us. "Been scavenging, have you?" he asked, squatting down and laughing. "Stalking a big old gecko, perhaps? Lost track of the time?"

He was right. I wasn't hungry, but not for the reasons he thought. It's not in a cat's nature to be too over-emotional, but how glad I was that it was never necessary to explain. I wasn't even sure if I would be *able* to explain.

And perhaps I didn't need to. I made a start on the herrings.

It was after we'd sailed before the extent of my "celebrity status", as the captain put it, *really* began to sink in. Though I had managed to avoid any involvement in anything to do with trunks, leads or collars while on land, it seemed I wasn't going to be able to escape entirely, as no sooner had we reached the open sea than Captain Kerans managed to collar *me* and affix the stiff new collar around my neck. He wasn't content with my just wearing it — I was made to pose with it for a series of photographs, too. "You'll be the star of Pathé news!" he assured me.

Then there was the news report that someone had brought on board just before we'd slipped, and which, during our usual church service a couple of days later, Lieutenant Hett had produced and read out to the crew.

"*Sailors get award,*" he began. "That's 'sailors' as in Simon and Peggy here, as opposed to you lot, obviously," he added, sweeping his gaze around the deck. "*Hong Kong: Able Seaman Simon and Guardsman Peggy received campaign ribbons on Saturday with all the modesty of heroes. In their case, it was a purr and a wag of the tail. As members of the crew of the British sloop Amethyst, during the dash down the Yangtse from communist captivity, they were honoured in a ceremony in the British Navy's Fleet Club, complete with honour guard.*

"*Said Petty Officer Griffiths, who officiated at the ceremony, to Peggy the dog: Guardsman Peggy for meritorious service on HMS Amethyst, is hereby awarded the distinguished Amethyst Campaign Ribbon.*

"*Simon the cat* — Yes, that's you, Simon. I *told* you you shouldn't have missed it — *got the same, word for* word, and this additional citation: 'Let it be known that though recovering from wounds, Simon did single-handed and unarmed hunt down and destroy Mao Tse-tung, a rat guilty of raiding food supplies.

"Another *Mao Tse-tung* is the leader of China's communists." He folded the paper and grinned. "Like we didn't know *that*, eh?"

But the piece in the newspaper was as nothing compared to the surprise that would greet me a few hours later.

With all the routines of heading to sea again taking priority over everything, once the service was over it was all hands to their duties. We were well out of the harbour and on our way to Singapore when Captain Kerans came and found me.

"Ah, *there* you are," he said, plucking me unceremoniously from his bunk. "Something told me I might find you here, you little scallywag. Come on. We're off to see Frank in the wardroom."

I had no idea why, but I didn't mind the interruption. Now we were back at sea I would have plenty of time for napping. It was a good feeling. A good feeling indeed.

We duly went down to the wardroom, Captain Kerans humming to himself as he carried me. It was good to see him so happy too.

But he stopped in the doorway. "Goodness me!" he exclaimed. "Look at this lot! Good Lord. What a thing, eh?"

As I was still half asleep, I wasn't quite sure what he was on about. He seemed to be referring to a number of sacks — bulging hemp sacks, of the kind that the post usually came in — that had presumably been brought in by the quarter-master before we'd sailed.

He put me down on the big wardroom table and turned to Frank. "This lot is really *all* for Simon?"

Frank nodded. "Aye aye, sir. The lot. All been sorted already. And you're right. You *wouldn't* credit it, would you?"

Yes, I thought, padding across the table for a better look, *but what is it? What's this "lot" that he's on about?* Because I'd missed most of what Frank would probably call the "carryings-on", I had only the vaguest idea what they were talking about. And even less about what might be in the sacks.

Tins of sardines, hopefully. If they had been delivered here for me, there was a chance of that, wasn't there? I licked my lips. Tins and tins and tins of sardines, if I was lucky. And if I was even *more* lucky, there might be some cream in there too. For all Captain Kerans kept saying I looked "like the cat that got the cream" lately, I'd seen nothing in the way of cream — precious little in the way of milk, even — since we'd left Shanghai for Nanking all those months ago.

I could already feel my mouth watering at the prospect of my fond imaginings, but no one seemed much inclined to look for any. Instead, Frank pulled a clutch of papers from the top of one of the sacks, and started looking through them with what appeared to be great amusement.

He then pulled out another handful and Captain Kerans joined in too, wrestling out another wodge of them himself. "Well, I've seen everything now, Coxswain," he said, chuckling to himself and then waggling one of my ear tips. "I've seen a very great deal in my time in the Senior Service but I don't think I've ever seen anything quite like *this* before. Who could ever have imagined it?" he asked Frank. "Fancy. I really have never seen *anything* quite like it."

He thrust one of the papers under my nose. I was washing my whiskers — might as well, I thought, while they busied themselves in *not* finding any sardines — but the paper jiggled in front of me seemed at least worth a sniff. Then I realised what it was: it was post. It was letters. Just like the sacks of them that used to reach the *Amethyst* via the supply ships and, latterly, while we were marooned up the Yangtse, via the sampan or landing craft that used to bring them sporadically, and which always caused such a great fuss.

Post was important. I knew that. It had always been important. It was one of the things that kept the crew happy and boosted morale — though I was so often privy to it having quite the opposite effect (at least in private) that, for all that my human friends loved to receive it, I didn't trust the business of post quite as much as I might have.

I sniffed the letter carefully. "Yes, you're absolutely right," Captain Kerans said, looking pleased with himself. "That's *you*, little feller. *Able Seacat Simon*, is what it says there." He ran his finger along the writing. "*Care of HMS* Amethyst, *Hong Kong*. As does this," he added, flipping through the rest of the pile in his hand. "As does this, as does this, as does this. They are *all* for you." He scratched his head again. "Honestly, Frank, really. Who'd have *thought* it? This little fellow here has obviously captured quite a few hearts!"

"I'll say so, sir," agreed Frank. He was still busy with his own sack and was now pushing his arm halfway down it. I wasn't altogether sure what the captain meant. Captured hearts? Because, confused though I was, I'd at least worked out one thing: that the contents of the sacks seemed very likely to be related to the masses of people who'd come to greet us at the quayside on the morning we'd docked, and who'd continued appearing right up until we'd left Hong Kong. And related to the collar, and the ceremony I'd been at pains to avoid attending, and to the piece in the newspaper about Mao Tse-tung.

I eyed the sack Frank was still riffling through hopefully. Perhaps he had found some sardines at last.

Apparently not. Well, at least, I doubted it, because what now appeared in his hand was a strange-looking package, wrapped in brightly patterned paper, and which looked as much like a tin of sardines as I did. "Permission to open it, sir?" he asked the captain.

"Of course, Frank, go ahead. I'm sure Simon'll be keen to see what it is, won't you, feller?"

Which I was, well, a little. I certainly liked the paper, which crackled pleasingly and looked fairly interesting. But no sooner had I worked out that there was unquestionably no fish in it than something flew from

Frank's hand, wheeled high overhead, and landed with a flump on my head.

It wasn't hard enough to hurt, but it was something of a shock so, though I was aware they found it funny, I immediately launched myself at it and (as a cat has to do in such situations, *always*) held it tight between my front paws, clamped my jaws around what appeared to be its neck, and then proceeded to attack it with my hind legs.

"Well, that's apt," the captain said, grabbing the other end of it and tugging, which seemed no sort of thing for the captain to be doing and definitely something he had never tried to do with any rat I'd presented him with. So I let the prey go, not least because it didn't even seem to be wriggling. Was it dead? I felt suspicious. Had it ever been alive?

I pulled back. I sat on my haunches, and took a better, more considered look at it. Until Captain Kerans picked it up and tried to rub it against my nose. I didn't hiss — that would be rude — but I certainly shuffled back a bit. Whatever this thing was, one thing was very clear now. It definitely wasn't any kind of food or animal.

Frank laughed. "You know what, sir, thinking about it, I wonder if our Simon has ever even *seen* a cuddly toy before. I don't reckon so, do you?"

"I suspect you might be right," the captain said, waggling it in front of me again. "It's a *mouse*, Simon," he said. "See? A mouse for you to *play* with. Squeak squeak!"

Then he shook his head. "As if he's in need of such diversions round here, eh? Still, it's jolly nice. And it's the thought that counts, obviously. He's not going to have much access to rats in quarantine, after all. I tell you what, Frank, we'll need to put someone in charge of this. If this is the shape of things to come, there'll be a lot more of the same before we finally make Plymouth. And we must do the decent thing and keep a record. Catalogue what's received. Get some photographs taken. I've a feeling the fourth estate will be interested in this, what with the Dickin thing, don't you? Tell you what," he said, having popped the post he'd pulled out back in the sack. "Have a word with Lieutenant Hett; see if he'd like to take charge of this. Just the job for him. Don't you think? Something to keep him amused on the long journey home."

I got another bat on the head then, with the thing which was definitely *not* a mouse. "So now you even have your own official Ship's Cat Officer, Simon! How about that?" said the captain.

But it was what Frank said next that really floored me. "And how about this lot?" he asked the captain, gesturing to another bulging sack.

"Er . . . what? You mean there's more?"

Frank nodded. "This lot's been sent for Peggy. Wasn't sure what best to do with it all now she's gone, sir."

"Of course," he said. "Well, let me think. Have it dropped off at Shanghai, perhaps?" Then he seemed to ponder for a moment. "On the other hand, doubt the purse strings will extend to having it shipped back to her in Hong Kong . . . Not given that it was the purse strings that had us leave her there in the first place, eh? No, on balance, we'll just hang on to it. That would seem to be the best thing. Leave it with Lieutenant Hett. Perhaps the gifts could go to the PDSA."

"Good idea, sir," said Frank. "Righty ho." Then he turned to me. "So, young Simon, me lad. Wonder what other delights are going to be here for you?"

I could only stare at him, the "cuddly toy" (which wasn't cuddly in the least bit) forgotten. Peggy gone? Peggy gone? Gone where?

CHAPTER
TWENTY-ONE

Bay of Biscay, 1 November 1949

It took three months for us to sail to England, time which I spent as I'd always done; maintaining my watches, keeping the (now thankfully much smaller) rat population in check and wherever possible finding a billet in a warm, welcoming bunk or hammock, particularly as the temperature began dropping, and the thing they called "taters" and "parky" and something about "brass monkeys" began to take on substance and shape.

Peggy had indeed gone, and the ship felt all the quieter and sadder for it. I kept listening for her bark, or bracing myself for her imminent arrival, or expecting her to appear around the corners of passageways, bounding along and prancing about and extremely keen to lick me, her tail thwacking back and forth like a mast in a gale. Then I'd remember that she wouldn't, because something called the "purse strings" meant she had been found another home, and in Hong Kong, which was strange and unsettling.

As for the why, what about Petty Officer Griffiths, who was the one who'd brought her on board? She'd been his dog originally. So how did he feel about it? With no answer forthcoming, I could only wonder about it. And wonder I did. How did *Peggy* feel about it? I missed her.

For the most part, the time passed easily, with the ship shipshape, the men occupied and the atmosphere largely happy. The traumas we'd all been through were fading thankfully away, though at the same time, albeit curiously, they worked an unlikely magic in making everyone appreciate how lucky we were.

But the closer we got to the place almost everyone called home, the more I became aware that something significant might be happening — something that I might not quite like. I could sense it, in the same way that cats can sense most things, and though I didn't know what it was, I was about to find out.

"I know how you're going to feel, Blackie," Jack was explaining, on the morning of our arrival. It was past eight o'clock but, in this curious part of the world, still quite dark. "You're going to feel like we've abandoned you. But we haven't," he said. "Not a bit of it, okay? It's just that there's nothing we can do about it. There's no getting round quarantine, I'm afraid. The law's the law, and there's no way around the law once we're home, even if you are the most famous cat in the world."

It was a curious business, sitting in the mess with so many of my friends, knowing this was the last day, perhaps for a long time, that we'd all be at sea together.

206

We were within "spitting" distance, as Frank would say. I wished we weren't.

We'd left Gibraltar the previous day and were now making good speed to Devonport, where everyone kept saying we were going to have ourselves a welcome to rival all the welcomes we'd already had put together. We were returning as heroes, and the "world and his wife" would be waiting there to greet us, which, though it clearly made my friends happy in the utmost — which of course made *me* happy — was increasingly making me feel sad for myself, because it reminded me that my home was *here*.

Back in Hong Kong, we had already been greeted by more people than I had ever seen together in one place. It had been much the same ever since. We'd stopped at so many ports along the way, it was hard to keep track of them — Singapore, Penang, Colombo, Aden and Port Said — where Frank was reunited with his son, and had to try so hard not to cry.

Then it was Malta, and most recently Gibraltar. I'd not gone ashore — after Hong Kong, I didn't think I'd better wander off again, just in case — but each dock would still have a place in my memory because each had smelled different, looked different, felt different. In one aspect, each had been much like the one before it; we'd leave the open sea only to have it replaced by another; a sea of cheering humans, the warmth in their smiles, waves and welcomes unwavering, whatever the vagaries of the weather.

But since leaving Gibraltar, something very worrying had started happening; something that was beginning to make me question my previous assumption that, once the *Amethyst* had been repaired, and the crew had seen their families, we'd be off to our next posting on the South China Seas.

The worry was that strange new word "quarantine". That curious word that Captain Kerans had first mentioned just as we'd left Hong Kong, and which I wished I had paid a great deal more attention to. This strange, worrying place where there'd be no rats to hunt — that much I had at least recalled.

I'd been hearing the word "quarantine" here and there ever since. Not to me, particularly, but always in tones that made me sure it was something not so much to be excited about, but be borne.

I stood up on Jack's lap now, arched my back and had a stretch, then settled down again and, because I knew he was in his best togs today, took care not to knead my front claws on his knees.

"Daft, ain't it?" said Martin, who was similarly scrubbed up. The whole crew were, because once we docked, the ship's company were going on parade again — their last in a run of them (I'd never seen so much spit-and-polishing) this one, the main one, through the streets of Plymouth. "You'd think they'd make an exception for him, wouldn't you?" he argued. "I mean it's not like he's going to be off being someone's pet an' that, is it? Not like he couldn't just stick around with one of us till we're off on our travels again."

"Yeah, but where?" Jack said. "Someone would have to take him home, wouldn't they? You know, back out into civvy street. And you'd *hate* that, you would,

Blackie, trust me," he told me, running a big hand down my back. "Now you've got your sea legs, I reckon you'd find it pretty miserable. All those other cats, for one thing . . ."

"Oh, I don't know," said Martin, grinning. "Who's to say he wouldn't meet a nice lady cat? Being such a good-looking tom now, and all."

"Not to mention a war hero," Paddy pointed out, while I was still trying to work out if I was to be given yet *another* name. Tom? Where had Tom come from?

"Hey, Blackie, mate, that's a point," said Jack. "You can show all the girls your medal!"

I had no idea why, but they seemed to find this extremely funny, because they laughed so much that they all fell about the mess and doubled up, and Jack's lap suddenly became a wild, stormy sea. In fact, I only clung on till he choked on his ciggy, upon which I had to leap off and retire to a safe distance till he finished the resultant coughing fit.

He soon scooped me up again, and I wished so much that I could go home with him. With *any* of them. I'd be proud to. And yet it seemed I couldn't. It was becoming chillingly clear that I wouldn't be allowed to.

"Tell you what, though," Jack said, cuddling me, "we're going to miss you something awful. 'T ain't right, is it? You being packed off like this. Perhaps Peggy got the best of it. But then, you're a hero now, aren't you? No question of not bringing *you* home. But don't you worry, Blackie — they'll make such a fuss of you once you're there, you'll see. Give you a proper hero's welcome. You'll be spoiled rotten by all those kennel maids. Just you wait. And we won't leave you high and dry, mate," he added, tugging on one of my front paws. "A few of the lads don't live so far away from where they'll be taking you, me included. We'll come visit you, okay? Promise. So you'll have plenty of visitors to look forward to. You'll see — those six months will fly by in a flash. Even if it's that long, and I reckon it probably won't be. You wait, you'll pass muster with the powers that be and then we'll be all of us — well, most of us, I reckon — back to sea."

I tried to take this all in. In what sense might Peggy have had the best of it? What was the worst of it, then? What were they sending me to? If I was going there, I was going there, so I tried to think like Jack did. Tried to remember I must make the best of it. Tried to remember what Captain Griffiths had once said to me about both sailors and cats being so adaptable. To be reassured that my friends *would* come and visit me, just as they promised. That the time would pass quickly. That the kennel maids — whoever they were — would indeed make a fuss of me. But *six months*. Six whole *months*. That was how long he'd said it might be, hadn't he? We'd been 101 days aground at Rose Island — which was barely half that. And if that had felt like forever and a day — which was how I remembered Jack himself had put it — then how long would my spell in the quarantine place feel?

I could hardly bear to think about it.

We were due to dock in Plymouth late morning. As we continued north, through a choppy, unfamiliar sea, I

210

could sense a lifting of spirits around me the like of which I didn't think I'd seen before, the men laughing and joshing with each other as we carved through the water, wearing our battle scars, as the captain put it, like bunting. There was much talk of things that were entirely new and strange to me. Talk of "Blighty" and "sweethearts" and "proper ale on draught, finally", none of which — however hard I tried — I could understand, let alone share. I could only get the sense that, for most of the men, this place called Plymouth was a "coming to" rather than a "leaving from" kind of city; that there were loved ones here, precious humans, some of whose pictures I'd seen often, and who would apparently be waiting excitedly to greet them when we finally drew alongside wharf six.

I thought back to Stonecutters Island, the place where I'd been born, and tried to put myself in their shoes. How wonderful it must be for my shipmates, after everything that they'd been through, to know that soon they might catch a glimpse of the people they'd missed so much, whose few letters they had read and reread so many times. I tried to imagine — though I chased the thought away as if vermin itself — what it would feel like to see my mum waiting there on the dockside for me too.

But that wasn't to be, and I had no choice but to accept it, however much I wished things were otherwise. I wished that we could sail right past this Plymouth (which from what I'd heard, and could now begin to see, looked cold and grey and regularly beset by sheets of heavy rain) and just head away again, fast, back out to the only home I now knew; the sea.

Instead I was bound for "quarantine". I kept hearing the word in my head over and over again. Quarantine. *Qu-ar-ant-ine*. It was such a strange word; a word I'd never heard before the captain had mentioned it. And I was no nearer to understanding it when Jack had said it either. Where was quarantine? *What* was quarantine? In what way did you go "into" it? And what was an animal supposed to do when it got there? For, from what Jack had half-explained, that much did seem to be clear. That only the animals from the *Amethyst* had to go in there — and since Peggy was longer there, she didn't have to — and that, given what I'd been through, I'd be treated like a king. But I didn't feel any the wiser about *why* we had to go there, or what naval duties might be required of me when I got there. If they didn't have a rat problem, perhaps they had another. Plagues of lizards, perhaps? Voles? I didn't think so, or else, why would they have needed Peggy? Peggy could no more catch a vole than her own tail. Was that why she'd left the *Amethyst*? Because they hadn't needed her in quarantine? That was still a mystery to me, too. And I was completely at a loss to know what I'd have to do in order to "pass muster". Only that it was "the law", and as Jack had made clear, no one — man or animal — was above *that*.

I tried to think it through logically; make some sense of why it had to happen, when, strictly speaking, I had been deemed "above" the law when on board the

212

Amethyst. I knew that because I'd heard it said more than once by my beloved Captain Griffiths. But what did it *mean*? I tried to rack my brains, to see if I could fathom it. If I remembered rightly, he'd said something about it when I walked over his new charts with wet paws one day — which now felt like such a very long time ago. "Look at this one," he'd said to Lieutenant Weston, who was working on them with him. "Bold as you like! Cock of the walk!" Then he'd shaken his head. "Mark my words, Number One, he thinks he's above the law, that one. Look at him! If he was a rating — are you listening, Simon? I said if you were one of my ratings I'd have you on a charge, you hear that? Put on deck-mopping duty —" He'd paused then and chuckled. "Or strung up against the mast and soundly thrashed with a cat-o'-nine tails! Yes, you heard right — a *cat*-o'-nine tails!" Then he'd thrown his head back and laughed. "And I'd have yours for good measure, you mucky pup!"

That had always been the thing about Captain Griffiths: he'd say one thing and do another, so sometimes you weren't sure where you were with him. Well, the men weren't — which was as it should have been — but I knew him rather better. So I wasn't in the least surprised when he'd picked me up, kissed my forehead and dropped me gently to the floor. It was what he'd often done, for all his blustering and huffing.

I tried to think how the two things might possibly be connected, but none of it, looking back now, made a

213

great deal of sense. Not least because, actually, it was Peggy who was the mucky pup.

So I wasn't any the wiser.

We docked at Devonport on schedule, and I had my first proper look at the place all my friends seemed to yearn for so much; the place about which they'd always talked so long and lovingly; the place which a lot of them had fought to protect.

I watched it fill the horizon from my newest favourite viewpoint (the stowage box on the upper foredeck, which was sheltered from the worst of the wind by the starboard whaler) and tried to feel the same sense of excited anticipation.

But it was difficult. It was nothing like the place where I'd been born. Unlike in Hong Kong, where the mountains rose behind us so magnificently, the land beyond the dock here was indistinct, flat and grey. It seemed to hug the earth rather than rise from it, as if anxious not to show itself. Such features as were visible all seemed to merge into one another, melting into, rather than meeting, the dingy smear of sky. There was little light, little colour; just the rain sliding down on us. This rain fell not so different from the way it had when we were trapped halfway up the Yangtse — out of a sky that was heavy with as yet unshed water. But, just as I had imagined from what I'd learned, it was not nearly as warm. All of which made it equally difficult for me to warm *to* the place. *Rain will come, kitten, I remembered, and you won't like it one bit.* Here, would it ever go away?

214

But as we approached, the warmth came to us in other ways. As we neared the harbour, it was as if the whole world had come to greet us; we were joined by a flotilla of all sorts of craft, their decks alive with sailors of all kinds. Boats and ships, big and small, were soon everywhere around us, while above us half a dozen planes swooped and dipped and soared, signalling their approval through the roaring of their engines.

The welcome on the dock was as warm as the Plymouth air was cold, with people stretching almost as far as the eye could see. And not just at the wharfside — every structure that had space on which to stand held yet more people, anxious to better see.

As we pulled alongside the wharf, to such a cacophony of cheering, to such a bright ocean of smiles, my friends' happiness began to rub off on me.

Not that I didn't have my wits about me, too. I had never seen so many humans crammed into such a small space, and experience had by now shown me that this could mean only one thing: that if I didn't make myself scarce they would soon all come swarming aboard and overwhelm me.

And come aboard they did, in their droves. For a while, it was impossible to avoid the crush and chaos, because Captain Kerans seemed determined to make me part of the celebrations, particularly when it became clear that everyone wanted to take my picture.

But there was the taking of pictures and the taking of pictures, and this was nothing like the picture-taking I had known. There were cameras everywhere, which didn't in itself worry me unduly; I'd long since got used to having my picture taken at sea, and had coped with all the people wanting them in Hong Kong. But here it seemed tenfold — like no other port before it. Many of the cameras were held by shouting, jostling men; men who seemed not to care about pushing in front of one another in order to shove their enormous lenses in my face, and, with a terrifying "pop!", blind me with hot white light.

There was nothing to be done but grit my teeth and get on with it, just as Captain Griffiths had always told me. And as I was held fast in the captain's arms, there was little I could practically do in any case, at least for the moment; to try to wriggle free from him would have been insubordinate in the extreme, particularly when he was recounting to everyone around us what heroes both Peggy and I had been.

But I think he sensed my discomfort. I could tell by the way he held me, and no sooner had the flashes begun popping in earnest than a lady stepped aboard — one whose face I thought I recognised — who, at a nod from Captain Kerans, held out her arms to me, scooping me up against her shoulder. She immediately bore me away along the nearest gangway, off the deck, away from all the crush and noise.

"Poor Simon," she whispered, speaking almost as if she knew me. "This is getting all too much for you, isn't it? And I'm not surprised at all," she added, holding me out in front of her to make the usual thorough inspection. "My word, you're doing well!" she said. "Almost as good as new, eh? Look at those whiskers. I did so feel for you losing those whiskers. But here they are, all grown again. You're a sight for sore eyes, and I've half a mind to take you hostage. I expected you to be looking so much more sorry for yourself."

"Something of a miracle, if you ask me, Mrs Kerans," came a voice from behind us. The lady turned, me along with her, and agreed that it was.

It was Lieutenant Hett, my official Cat Officer, and he shook his head slightly. "Honestly, you should have seen the state of him," he said, coming up and scratching the fur behind my left ear. "Captain's cabin took a direct hit, so it really *is* a miracle. Not just the whiskers — no eyebrows either, and shrapnel wounds everywhere . . . Never thought he'd last the night, let alone make any sort of recovery. It's no word of exaggeration that we owe a very great deal to this little fellow. And to Peggy too, of course. The pair of them. But especially this one, what with the rats, and him being so badly injured. Talk about nine lives! Brave as a lion, too, aren't you, Blackie?" he added, chucking me under the chin and grinning. "I tell you, all this fuss — if that's what it's being called, and I'm guessing *you're* finding it a fuss, aren't you, feller? Well, it's no less then he deserves, it really isn't."

There was a sharp rap on the bulkhead by the open door at that moment.

"Captain's compliments, sir. Can you come along to the forward deck, sir? The Vice Admiral's just coming aboard."

"Of course," Lieutenant Hett said. "I'll be there right away."

"What about this little fellow?" Mrs Kerans asked, still petting me.

"Well, if you wouldn't mind popping him in the CO's cabin and shutting the door, that would be grand. You'll know where it is . . ."

She nodded. "Indeed I do."

And it seemed she did. I was so busy wondering how she knew her way around the *Amethyst* so well, that she'd done exactly that before I'd even got my bearings (much less crafted some plan to have her indeed take me hostage), her "It's been an honour to meet you finally, Simon," still ringing in my ears as she click-clacked her way back along the deck.

It was cool in the captain's cabin — perhaps a little too cool for my liking — and with the bunk stripped, the walls bare and the dust cover over his typewriter, the sense that it was no longer Captain Kerans' cabin but simply a compartment was heightened. It seemed almost inconceivable that I'd been in this very place when a shell had exploded into it. I looked across towards the door, which was still riddled with shrapnel holes to remind me, but now minus the caps that habitually hung from it. I wondered how long it would be before I saw it again.

Because my memory of that day had never properly returned to me, I could only imagine, rather than relive, the events of that morning, but it occurred to me that Captain Kerans' wife might have been right. Perhaps it was a miracle that I was still here, even with me being so blessed on the lives front.

But what now? I was suddenly anxious for the next thing to happen. The sooner the parade was over, the ship repaired, and I had "passed muster" in the thing called quarantine, the sooner we'd be reunited and back at sea again.

I could hear noises floating up to me; perhaps the crew were being assembled. Perhaps the parade through the streets of Plymouth was about to begin. I hopped up onto the captain's bunk and across to peer out of the scuttle, from where I had at least a partial view of events down on the quay.

There were indeed lots of things happening below me. Crowds moving along, opening up a route, the crew beginning to get into position, the cameras still popping, a marching band playing, flags waving everywhere, all of it so good to see. The air of joy and celebration was almost palpable — but at the same time, the sense of leaving, of my friends leaving me, was acute. I could hardly bear to watch as they marched away from me.

I turned away. I would take refuge in sleep, I decided. Take advantage of the peace and quiet and have forty winks. Since I was shut in here — itself peculiar, but I tried not to think about it — the captain's bunk, even minus its covers, would do nicely.

I'm not sure what made me pad back over to the scuttle then. The sound of the parade was growing fainter and fainter, so I'm not sure what instinct led me back for one last look. But it did, and I saw something on the quayside that made my blood run cold.

It was a man walking towards the *Amethyst*, carrying a cage.

CHAPTER
TWENTY-TWO

He was clad in a brown coat, and wore a hat of a type I hadn't seen before. I didn't take my eyes off him till he disappeared beneath me, up the gangway.

I knew I must be brave — hadn't Jack promised they would all come and visit me? But the cage was such a scary thing — such an unexpected horror — that I stayed where I was, still transfixed by the sight of it, long after I couldn't see it any more.

A *cage*. They were actually going to put me in a *cage*? It was almost too overwhelming to contemplate. Was this my immediate future? To be trapped in a cage? To become one of those wretched souls I'd seen in the Hong Kong markets, doomed to see out their days trapped behind bamboo bars? Was that what quarantine was going to be? A place where animals were held prisoner? For as long as it took them to pass muster with the powers that be? I wished so much that I could work out what that meant.

It was soon enough to send me into a flat spin of panic. I jumped down from the captain's bunk and hid away under it, squeezing into the scant space between the bed base and floor. Here I tried to think. Should I try to keep hidden? Would that be best? There were so many places and spaces to choose from, after all; so many secret nooks where no one bar the rats would be able to find me. But the idea seemed futile, even as I thought it, because what would be the point? The *Amethyst* was fast becoming a cold, empty vessel, with almost everyone I knew and loved already gone from it, all away down the wet streets, proud and happy. And without my friends, would I really be any better off than in quarantine? No, I wouldn't. Given that the *Amethyst* was now to go to a repair dock, which I knew was the plan, it would make it all the harder to be reunited with them. I'd have to scavenge for food again, leave the ship, live off my wits — become a stray again, in fact, which was the last thing I wanted. No. Despite the cage, I must, I *must*, be brave.

So when the door opened, revealing the captain's wife and the man in the brown coat, I squeezed back out again and allowed him to take me. When he put me in the cage — which smelled of something alien and bitter and immediately made me gag — I didn't even hiss at him. I was an able seacat, and I had to be strong now.

We left the ship just as the sound of the parade melted away altogether, and the few remaining well-wishers peeled away too. The sky was still dark as if dusk was falling soon, though it wasn't even close. As the man carried me down the gangway I had to concentrate hard not to panic, putting all my energies into trying to keep my balance as the cage, with me in it, jiggled and swung at his side, and thumped against the side of his leg.

"You'll be fine," he said. "There, there," he said. "There's a good boy," he said. I was reassured that he said all this not unkindly. But then he opened the back of his van, filling my nose with foul, confusing odours, placed the cage inside, then shut me in the dark. "Go to sleep now, little fellow," he said as he shut the door behind me. I knew I wouldn't.

The journey was long. Oh, so long. As long as one of Jack's watches. And with nothing to look at bar a glimpse of darkening sky through the little square scuttle, I could only retreat into my thoughts. I was taken back to my first days aboard the *Amethyst* immediately: the same wobbly weakness, the same nagging queasiness. I had travelled what must have been thousands of miles across the ocean, and, apart from those first days when I struggled to keep my feet where my brain said the deck was, I hadn't felt sick like this before.

It was such a long journey that at one point we stopped. The man came to "see" to me — or so he told me — to give me a small bowl of water and a cuddle, standing on a grassy strip at the side of a busy road.

He put me back in then. Shut the cage door, which was made of the same wire as the rest of it, then disappeared out of sight, the back doors of the van still hanging open. I stared out into the half-light, feeling perplexed and morose and unsettled, with the cars thundering past, kicking up spray. I decided I hated roads just as much as I ever had.

222

I must have slept then, because I woke with a start, hearing a noise. Light flooded in. A bright light, like a searchlight, which dazzled and confused me. A light not like the moon — too close, too bright, too startling — radiating down from above and making rods of the raindrops which were falling steadily and thickly on the ground.

"Come on, lad," said a new voice. Then, "Thanks. You must be exhausted. This flipping weather. Cats and dogs, eh?" This to the man, who'd come back into view again. A high voice. Soft and welcoming. A woman's. "Long old trip. Still, you're here now. Shall I make you a cuppa? Let's get him in and then I'll go and put the kettle on."

It was the woman who carried me, cooing in gentle, friendly tones. I tried to feel reassured by it, shaking the sleep from my head, as the cage was borne steadily — carefully, gently — up a path, lined with more grass, to a large wooden door.

"There," she said as we reached it, speaking down to me in the cage. "Our precious cargo delivered. We're so excited to have you! Everyone's so looking forward to meeting you. But first something to eat, yes? Poor mite. You must be hungry. And bewildered too, I'll bet. You must be wondering what on earth's going on, eh? But there's nothing to be afraid of." She set the cage down on a table. Then her face loomed. A round face. A pale face. A friendly face. I couldn't stop shaking, even so.

I was taken, still in the cage, to another compartment, and the first thing that struck me was the absence of metal. It was a huge compartment. Almost as big as the place in the picture in the paper, from where Peggy had received our awards. *Oh, Peggy,* I thought, feeling unbearably lonely suddenly. Everything would be so much better if Peggy was with me. I missed the smell of her. I missed her barking. I missed the sound of her sleepy whimpers — chasing rabbits in her dreams, Jack had told me. I missed the thump of her tail when it struck a piece of canvas. I even missed the sudden sprays of water when she'd been horsing around on deck and got herself drenched by the mops and the buckets. Peggy would be fine here, and I missed her so much.

But I knew I must rally and trust in the woman's gentle tones. I was welcome. She'd told me. No one wished me any harm here. On the contrary; within minutes half a dozen people had clustered round me, one wondering if they should get me out and "take a proper look at me", or leave me. Or feed me. Or simply transfer me, as it was late, to the "cattery" straight away — which word sent me all into a spin once again.

In the end it was decided that, since everyone wanted to cuddle me, the best thing would be to take me out and do so. I was passed around, fussed over, and declared to be a hero. That same word again and again, and again, always said so reverentially.

So I tried hard not to quake. Tried to purr. Tried to please them. And I did rally, even when I was taken to another place — a *room* (that was their word for it) that was apparently going to be my home. It was almost all white, and at first sight, a more reassuring place to me:

224

angular, functional, and reassuringly metal. It smelled a little like the *Amethyst*'s sick bay.

Less reassuringly, I then saw where I was going to be billeted, which was a smaller compartment within it. It was still a cage, I supposed, but a much bigger one than I'd come in. It had a human-sized wire door, beyond which lay a basket — "This is your bed, Simon. Isn't it cosy?" said the lady — and beyond that, a rectangular tray which was filled with tiny pebbles, and to the side a brace of small shallow bowls, one containing water, the other empty.

I looked first at the "bed", which was not like any bed I'd ever slept on, then up above it, where, to my immense relief, I saw there was a high place. I scampered up a gangway that seemed there specifically to take me to it, and there I stayed, trying to trick my brain into believing I was not where I was. That I had once again boarded the *Amethyst*, and we were sailing. And then, remembering that sleep was so often the best refuge, I slept.

On second inspection, just before sunrise the following morning, quarantine looked less terrifying than I'd first expected. Yes it was a strange place, and, despite the gangway, very different from the *Amethyst*, but not so different that it felt completely alien. And though the sky was still grey, and seemed to hang so low above me, there was at least a window that enabled me to see it.

It was odd knowing the world outside the window felt like home for most of my human friends, as, to me, it looked barren and strange. The skeletal trees here were nothing like banyans or tamarinds. They seemed to claw upwards towards the sky, for one thing, though below them there was enough green to cheer me up a bit. Not on the trees, but it did seem to carpet almost everywhere. When we arrived, and I'd finally been freed from the cage, it had felt strangely reminiscent of the garden around the old lady's house.

I remembered what the man in the brown coat had said to me when we'd arrived here. "You'll be treated like a king here, me little laddo," he'd reassured me. "Just you wait — you'll be the bee's knees *and* the bug's elbows!"

I had no idea what he meant then, and I still didn't now. But remembering it, and particularly the way he'd said it, made me resolute. I must remember there was nothing to fear here. So, mindful of Captain Griffiths, who had always led by example, I duly settled in and got on with it.

And on one level, it was an easy thing to do. The man in the brown coat had been right about my welcome. However strange my new home, I couldn't have been treated with more kindness, particularly by the lady who'd greeted me when I'd arrived. Her name was Joan, she said, and she'd been given special responsibility for me.

Every day — twice a day, in fact — post arrived for me. Such a lot of post! Being mindful of how happy post made my shipmates, I decided the post was yet another thing to reassure me. I was thought about. I was missed. I was loved.

There were sacks and sacks of letters, of the kind I'd first seen in the wardroom, and I wished Lieutenant Hett could be with me to share them. There were more cuddly toys, things to play with, and enticing new things to eat. There were also visitors — though often strangers, who would sometimes overwhelm me. I was used to my shipmates, every last lovely man jack of them, but the seemingly endless procession of new faces (albeit smiling ones, with nothing but praise for me) began to stress me and make me keen, unbelievably, for the sanctuary of my cage. And for my high place, for which I was very grateful.

I was also visited, to my joy, by a few crew members. Not Jack, because Jack's home on dry land was several hundred miles away. But I saw Frank and Sid, and Lieutenant Hett, and though I hated that feeling when I watched them leave the building again, it was enough to keep my spirits mostly buoyant.

Best of all, Captain Kerans and his wife, who was called Stephanie, visited twice, and on his second visit he promised me that, should it work out that way for whatever reason, I had a permanent home in England, with them. Which was a comfort, but at the same time, a worry as well. What about the *Amethyst*? Would I not be given another roving commission? Would I not be able to rejoin my ship and go to sea again?

I tried to put it out of my mind and find pleasure in each day — after all, I was being treated exactly as Jack predicted: given nice things to eat, made a great deal of fuss of and, best of all, I had Joan, who had already become a friend, and who spent a lot of time playing with me every day.

I was especially grateful to Joan. Because one thing did strike me, and it struck me very quickly; I finally understood the word "boredom". Without my friends and my work and the whole ship to roam, days were longer here, passing agonisingly slowly.

I remembered what Jack had told me the sailors sometimes did at such times. Mark a cross on a calendar as each day was done; create a line, then a block, then another, then another, till the days without crosses were almost none.

Perhaps I should do that, if only in my head. Mark a cross in my mind for every day that I spent here till the day came — and it would — when I finally passed muster and was allowed to pick up the thread of my seafaring life.

Because at those times between visitors, and when Joan was busy elsewhere, the time really did seem to crawl. So I snoozed — I had never done quite so much snoozing — and tried to remember how much I had to look forward to, not least the ceremony that Captain Kerans told me would take place in December, at which I'd formally be presented with a very important medal — the one I was to receive in place of the ribbon I'd been sent when we were back in Hong Kong.

Though I was grateful, I was privately bemused by it all. I had done nothing more than the job that had been expected of me from the outset; from when Captain Griffiths had given me my commission aboard the *Amethyst*, to take charge as best I could of the rats.

Everything else — all this talk of courage and gallantry, and of comforting my shipmates in troubled times — that was no more than I'd have done willingly *without* the commission. I had been given a wonderful opportunity, given friends and given hope. I had been reborn, almost — given a life I could never have dreamed of, and though the horror of that April day would stay with me also, I already felt so privileged; I had made friends, who I loved, and would continue to cherish and, most of all, I had escaped with my life and recovered, where many brave, decent men had not.

In short, more than anything, I had simply been lucky. If I'd seemed to have been in any way heroic, it was the least I could do — the *very* least I could do — as a mark of my gratitude.

Perhaps it was exhaustion — so many visitors, so many people, so many comings and goings. Or perhaps it was the fact that I no longer had a ship to wander around and the sea breeze to refresh me that, unaccustomed to the lassitude, I'd grown weary. I didn't know why or how, but something was wrong. Some sort of malaise seemed to take a grip of me.

It was late on one crisp, cold November afternoon that I began to feel unwell. Joan had brought me sardines, but I couldn't face eating, and milk, which I didn't want to drink.

"You're off colour, aren't you, pet?" she declared, looking anxious. Then she went off, at some speed, to fetch the man called the vet, who was like the doc, only he took care of animals.

I tried to stand up when she came back with him. I was always pleased to see him. He had hands as big as shovels, but you'd never have known it, he was always so gentle.

"Oh!" Joan said, as I stood, then I wobbled and fell back over. "You see?" she said. "He's not well at all."

The vet took hold of me and examined me on his big metal table, and even his gentle touch made me tremble. My skin felt all shivery, and my head felt all woozy. Joan was right. I really didn't feel well at all.

The vet took my temperature, and some blood — which I barely even noticed — then I was put to bed, where I slept for a bit. And when I woke, I heard his voice. He was standing outside my cage now, discussing me with Joan. I tried to look but my eyes kept flickering closed.

"It looks like a pretty nasty virus," the vet was telling her. "So he'll need to go into isolation, just to be on the safe side."

"Of course," I heard Joan say, in her gentle voice.

"I'm going to give him some drugs," the vet went on. "An injection and some tablets. The tablets to help him sleep. That's the best way."

He sighed then. "There's little else to be done, I'm afraid. As far as this ruddy virus goes, it's really up to him now."

I sensed Joan before I saw her; I felt the vibration in the air as the door opened, and her hand came across to stroke me. Then I heard her sigh as well, and the sound of it shook me to the core. "It's so unfair," she said. "After all the poor mite's been through. And him still so *young* . . ." She didn't say any more.

"Well, he's proved the odds wrong once," the vet said. "Let's hope he does the same again, eh? Wages the same war on this wretched virus as he seems to have done with all those rats . . ."

"I'll stay with him, tonight," Joan said at last, her voice low. "At least till he's gone off to sleep again. Well . . ." She paused. "Perhaps longer . . . Can't have him on his own. Not at a time like this. Oh, the poor little mite," she said again.

"Well," the vet said, "I commend you for your dedication." There was a pause, but again, I couldn't seem to keep my eyes open. "And I'm sure he'll pull through," the vet said eventually. "You know what they say about cats and their nine lives . . ."

CHAPTER
TWENTY-THREE

I had no idea what time it was when I woke up. The light spilling across the grass outside lent everything a pale luminescence, so it must be some time in the small hours of the morning, I supposed. I knew I'd slept for several hours — it had been perhaps the longest time I'd slept without waking for three days now; a deep, dreamless sleep, and one apparently untroubled by the fitful, and now feverish, nightmares that had dogged me since I'd left the *Amethyst* at Plymouth.

I was in a different room now. A smaller one, which was much more dimly lit. From where I lay, I could see though some glass doors to what looked like the quarantine garden. I was lying on my side, my head nestled on a square of folded muslin, and slightly to my right I could see Joan.

I was at first surprised she was still with me, because I'd slept for so long now, but then I realised that she was fast asleep herself, sitting in an armchair, her small hands clasped together loosely in her lap. I liked the vet's hands but I loved Joan's hands the best. They always smelled of honeysuckle and jasmine, and were the softest and gentlest I'd ever known.

232

I lay motionless for some time, taking stock of my surroundings, and making a mental assessment of how I was feeling. Not because I felt anxious about moving, as I had when I'd been injured on the Yangtse, but because, though I felt wide awake now, and seemed free of my fever, I also felt no pressing need to move anywhere. I was comfortable, relaxed, and could think of no particular reason to be anywhere other than I was, happy to let my body rest and leave my mind do the wandering.

I thought back to the events of the last couple of weeks. To the curious nature of being back on what my friends had called "dry land" but which had, for the most part, been anything but. As had often been the case when we'd been stranded on the Yangtse, this place — this patch of land my friends called home, and seemed to love so much — seemed endlessly beset by heavy rain.

It had been raining constantly, beating a tattoo on the window, the sound of it almost as mesmerising as Jack's Morse code machine. Only here, with no sun to suck it back up to make the clouds again, the rain lingered and seemed to cause everyone trouble. "Muddy feet! Muddy boots! Muddy paws! Blooming mud!" These were the words that had often drifted over to me as I dozed, along with other things that made no sense — and which I would spend hours pondering — such as the business of it being "too cold to snow." I was, I decided, settling in well.

I thought of the kindnesses shown to me, which had sometimes overwhelmed me, and of the letters and gifts

233

that were being sent to me, *still*. As if I had done something more than the men and dog I'd served with. Which I hadn't. I'd just done what I could. Which had always been the most — and least — I *could* do. It was beginning to become something of an embarrassment.

I thought mostly of my friends, and what they might be doing, and wondering if they might be thinking of me too.

I thought of Jack, and his "herrings in", and the long nights we spent together. Of how glad I was to hear he'd been decorated for his efforts — of how much of a hero and a true friend he had been.

I thought of gentle George Hickinbottom, who'd left the ship so long ago — was he at home with his cat, Sooty? I hoped so.

I thought of Captain Kerans, who'd brought us all to safety. How proud I felt to have him as my friend, and how much I looked forward to seeing him again.

I thought of Captain Griffiths, whom I'd loved and who'd given me my name. It was nice to think, even if our paths never crossed again, that my picture might end up on a bulkhead above his bed, and that I might be another memory in his heart.

Mostly, though, I found myself thinking increasingly of my mother, and of the cat's life she'd tried to prepare me for but which I'd never quite had. Was she still up there, looking down on me? Was she proud of me? Did she know I was now an able seacat? I realised how much I wanted to be reassured on all those points — perhaps a feeling at the heart of orphaned souls everywhere.

It was a clear evening, and from where I lay I could see enough of the night sky through the window to view a sprinkling of stars. They felt far away here — further than they'd ever felt before — and it struck me all at once that perhaps being in the middle of this land mass was the problem. I'd begun my life by the sea, and spent the rest of it on it. Perhaps dry land was not a good place for a cat like me to be.

I thought I might like to go and sit by the window. But, despite feeling so different, and so pain free, I wasn't sure I dared to — it having also come back to me just how much it had hurt when I'd come round after the shelling back in April. Yet my fever seemed to have dipped now, and my body felt relaxed, and it occurred to me that I might be well enough not only to move to the window, but to consider setting off on another journey.

You'll be back on board before you know it, old son. Captain Kerans had been clear on that point.

Wouldn't be the same without you, Blackie! Had that been Jack, or was it Frank?

Couldn't countenance it, Simon. You're one of us! Was that Lieutenant Hett? It was all becoming so blurred in my mind.

But when *would* I — would we — be back on board my beloved *Amethyst*? I didn't know. And neither did they. In the meantime, the feeling was growing ever stronger that I was not meant to stay here on dry land. That I didn't *want* to stay here any longer.

Then come to me.

I started. It was my mother's voice.

Come to me, kitten. Clear and strong now. *I want you to tell me all your tales.*

I opened my eyes. Strained to look. Strained to see as well as hear her. But the brightness of the moon, making everything gleam, was too strong for me to be able to see beyond it to the furthest stars. It was a full moon, and the light from it spilled across everything, streaming through the glass door, washing whitely over the linoleum, sculpting and painting everything with a luminous creamy brightness. It settled on Joan, on the table, on the cabinets and chair legs, catching fire here and there, wherever it met with something shiny, bathing everything it its warm benevolent glow.

And on me. I realised I was quite, quite recovered. No longer fearful. No longer parched. No longer pining for what had been, or worrying about what might yet not happen. No longer anxiously struggling against the illness the vet had told Joan in grave terms that I must fight as hard as I had fought the *Amethyst*'s rats.

Was that no longer true? Had the virus left my body? I stretched out a paw, tentatively at first, testing ligaments and tendons.

That's the way, kitten, I heard my mother say. *You're done with this life. Come to me. Come to me now. Come and tell me all your tales . . .*

I stretched another limb, feeling a new strength begin to flow through my body. Pinged my claws. Flicked my tail. Felt a breeze stir my whiskers. Felt a lightness of spirit I'd not felt in days.

I rose then. Another day, another journey, another place.

Another life to be lived, and so many stories to tell. I was ready to begin the next part of my adventure.

Epilogue

Simon (or Blackie, as he was known to most of the *Amethyst*'s crew) died on 28 November 1949, succumbing to enteritis, a complication of the virus he'd probably contracted at the quarantine centre he'd been sent to in Surrey. For a young cat to die of such a virus was very unusual, but it was suggested that perhaps he had been born with a weak heart and that his many injuries from the shelling, not to mention daily battles with large, aggressive rats, might also have taken their toll.

Members of the *Amethyst's* crew, who had been to visit him — including Captain Kerans and his wife — felt very differently. As did Telegraphist Jack French, who maintained that Simon's death was much more likely to be due to a broken heart, as a result of being separated from, and perhaps believing he had been abandoned by, the shipmates who, since Ordinary Seaman Hickinbottom had plucked him from the docks in Hong Kong's Stonecutters Island, had been the only family he'd ever known.

"I think Simon died because he lost the company of sailors," he is reported as saying. "He was quite content to be aboard the ship. They could quite easily have left him aboard the ship and he could have gone on to the next commission. I firmly believe he died of heartbreak. He pined away."

No one knew for sure how old Simon was at the time of his death, but it was believed that he was less than four years old, and probably much younger. It was tragically young for a cat to die, particularly one who'd displayed such devotion to his military duty, and who'd captured the hearts of a nation. The nation certainly mourned him; scores of condolence cards were sent to him, and he even had a tribute paid to him in the obituary pages of *Time* magazine. A few days later, his body wrapped in cotton wool and his tiny coffin draped in the Union Jack, he was laid to rest at plot 281 of the PDSA's pet cemetery in Ilford, after a funeral service with full Naval Honours.

Simon's Dickin medal — the only one ever awarded to a cat — was accepted on his behalf by Lieutenant Commander Kerans on 11 December, in the company of the officers and men of the *Amethyst*. It stayed on board the frigate till the ship was scrapped in the 1957, when it was moved to the Naval Trophy Store on HMS *Nelson*, in Portsmouth, before being auctioned off and sold to a collector in Canada.

The medal resurfaced again as recently as 1993, by which time Simon's story had become known throughout the world. And his celebrity — something he always shied away from — had obviously not waned; when it was auctioned by Christie's in 1993 with a guide price of around £3,000 to £5,000, it fetched

£23,467 — the highest amount for such a medal ever received.

Acknowledgements

No author works in isolation. Yes, we usually write in isolation, probably more than is healthy, but we invariably have company on our novel-writing journeys, in the form of fellow writers, whose work both informs and smooths the way.

I certainly couldn't have written this novel without help, and lots of it. From the web pages that visualised Stonecutters Island, to the diagrams of the (often mystifying) interiors of frigates, and with a special mention for the indefatigable Patrick Roberts, whose quest to discover Simon's full story, on www.purr-n-fur.org.uk, was the spark from which this novel was born. I am similarly grateful to www.maritimequest.com, which provided a wealth of information about the men involved in the Yangtse Incident. All hail the mighty internet, eh?

But there were two books, in particular, without which I would have floundered, the first being the diary of Coxwain Leslie Frank, which he kept religiously throughout the entire Yangtse Incident. An object lesson in the reality of the British stiff upper lip, it has been both a vital source of facts and figures, and an education.

I am also indebted to the journalist and author, Brian Izzard, whose new factual account, *Yangtse Incident: China and the ordeal of HMS Amethyst*, was another invaluable resource, not only because it contained previously undisclosed naval intelligence, but also because it was a cracking good read.

Yangtse River Incident 1949: The Diary of Coxswain Leslie Frank: HMS Amethyst — Yangtse River 19/4/49 to 31/7/49
Naval and Military Press 2003

Yangtse Incident: China and the ordeal of HMS Amethyst
Seaforth Publishing 2015

Other titles published by Ulverscroft:

THE MAGIC STRINGS OF FRANKIE PRESTO

Mitch Albom

At nine years old, Frankie Presto is sent to America in the bottom of a boat, his only possession an old guitar and six precious strings. Frankie's ability is unique, and his amazing journey weaves him through the musical landscape of the twentieth century, with his stunning talent impacting upon numerous stars along the way, including Elvis Presley, Carole King and even KISS. Frankie becomes a pop star himself. He makes records. He is adored. But his gift is also his burden, as he realises: through his music, he can actually affect people's futures — with one string turning blue whenever a life is altered. Then, at the height of his popularity, Frankie Presto vanishes, and his legend grows. Only decades later does he reappear to change one last life . . .

HOW TO MEASURE A COW

Margaret Forster

Tara Fraser leaves London to start a new life in a Cumbrian town selected at random. She plans to obliterate her past, which contains a shocking event that had serious consequences, by becoming a completely different personality from her previous volatile self. She is going to be quiet — even dull, and very private. But one of her new neighbours, Nancy, is intrigued by her, and wants to become her friend. Equally determined not to be discarded are three old friends who Tara feels let her down when she most needed them. Tara fights to keep herself to herself; but can she do it? And does she really want to? Slowly, reluctantly, she discovers that her attempts to suppress the past and reject other people are downright dangerous . . .